Mr Fluff

AND HIS MAGICAL ADVENTURES
IN THE ENCHANTED FOREST.

Mr Fluff

AND HIS MAGICAL ADVENTURES
IN THE ENCHANTED FOREST.

VERONICA KELLY

authorHOUSE®

AuthorHouse™ UK Ltd.
1663 Liberty Drive
Bloomington, IN 47403 USA
www.authorhouse.co.uk
Phone: 0800.197.4150

Published by AuthorHouse 06/10/2014

ISBN: 978-1-4969-8337-4 (sc)
ISBN: 978-1-4969-8338-1 (e)

Any people depicted in stock imagery provided by Thinkstock are models, and such images are being used for illustrative purposes only. Certain stock imagery © Thinkstock.

This book is printed on acid-free paper.

Contents

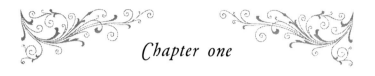

Chapter one

MR FLUFF AND THE MAGIC ROSE

$\mathcal{M}$r Fluff was a bright fat yellow and orange moth caterpillar. He was very fluffy with white spots and a black along his back. He was a Sycamore moth who loved eating chestnuts and other leaves of the trees. His favourite wish was not to become a moth at all. He wanted to be a beautiful butterfly. So he eats as much food as possible. All the other fairies had watched this big caterpillar eat as much food in the horse chestnut tree as he could. One naughty fairy put a spell on the caterpillar. His little face appeared to be very dainty and he could find out that he could talk to this small flying people. It was quite a noisy forest full of wonderful things. At night time he wriggled out of his lodgings and he glowed very much in the dark! His tail was truly a bright orange colour that lit brightly.

In the night Mr Fluff found himself wondering so far away from his Lodgings that he ended up crawling up an oak tree. The tree could feel something tickling his great big trunk. The trees eyes looked down below to see a tiny fluffy thing with a face. "Looks like the naughty fairies had put a spell on you" said the Oak tree.

"What? Said Mr Fluff to the tree.

"Someone has turned you into an unusual fluffy caterpillar"

"Silly flying fairies!" remarked the caterpillar. "I'm going to be a beautiful butterfly when I hatch out next spring!"

Mr Fluff decided to stay in the oak tree nibbling at a few leaves. The tree could hear him crunching for most of the evening. That the tree spotted a very bright rose bush in the distance of someone's garden. It belonged to a very good witch called Hazel who had just purchased her house, for a good sum of money. What a delightful surprise to tempt that munching caterpillar to get it on that rose bush, thought the Oak tree smiling with a grin.

"My little fluffy friend" said the tree. The caterpillar stopped munching at the trees juiciest leaves. With the trees looking just a bit annoyed at what speed that little thing was eating. Soon the caterpillar stopped and yawned and curled up in one of the leaves. He remained there for a few days' munching at the leaves for a long while.

Mr Fluff had found himself a hollow in the oak tree while wriggling quite high in the oak itself. The tree had dozed off into a sleep till mid afternoon. He had known that little thing had been there for quite a long time. He was quite a big caterpillar with a fairy face.

One day the tree told him that if you looked in someone's nice flowered garden, there is a nice rose bush that you could nibble at! The caterpillar looked into the garden and he lost his balance seeing a magic rose bush.

That same evening that rose bush, had bloomed all its roses for the witch Hazel. She popped out of her nice little cottage to collect a few magic petals to make some kind of magic spell.

The magic rose bush showed all its magic colours like a rainbow. This caught the attention of the fluffy caterpillar. Mr Fluff yawned as he wriggled from his cosy spot, and tried to wriggle down the tree. He was licking his lips with such excitement, that he tumbled right down to the bottom of the oak tree.

"You poor little soul" said the tree.

Mr Fluff found himself at the bottom of the oak tree and he told the tree he was ok and not hurt. So off he went to visit this beautiful garden full of flowers and that gorgeous rose bush. So he found the rose bush and wriggled up it to try a small bite of the petals. It tasted so delicious and fruity that he eat two petals and almost fell asleep in the rose. The witch came out into her garden to look at her roses. She spotted something very orange, and fluffy all curled up in a big ball.

"My, what a big orange caterpillar!" she said. She thought that she would leave the little thing alone.

Mr Fluff woke up with a surprise to see someone peering at the rose, and him. The witch and her mother giggled at the tiny caterpillar and saw his tiny little face. The little caterpillar saw the witch and her mother looking inside other roses for other caterpillars. It seemed that he was the only one. The rose bush had scattered some gold magic dust on the caterpillar, and Mr Fluff sneezed. He almost blew himself off the rose bush. The witch turned around as she was admiring her newly planted pots with geraniums with bright red flowers. When the rose bush giggled about what had landed in its magic rose. The witch thought she was hearing things. As you see, that nice cottage was built in an enchanted part of the forest. She had heard about some strange things in that part, but not much fairies that did some spells in the summer on some caterpillars. Mr Fluff decided to wriggle home to his beloved Oak tree. So off he went down the stem of the rose bush, covered in magic gold dust and over the garden wall, feeling rather tired and full over his meal. Mr Fluff stopped for awhile for a rest, in just a short distance from the oak tree and sneezed again and the gold dust went up his nose!

Soon he spotted the old oak snoring away. Mr Fluff went up its trunk to pop into the hollow. He had found himself such a cosy spot that he was ready to weave himself a silken bed. He made himself a fine bed of silk and soon fell into a magic deep spell cast by those naughty fairies.

Soon the summer had gone and Mr Fluff was fast asleep in a magic cocoon. The autumn had come. So the tree had shed some leaves. The tree had seen many tiny little things buzz around his branches, with birds and fairies gathering some leaves that had fallen down to the ground. The tree, knew something magically was going off. That the little caterpillar might turn into something else, but not a moth! The fairies did scatter some fairy dust in the hollow of the tree, and it was so pretty. That they also did it all around that caterpillar!

The winter came, covering the land in a thick carpet of snow. The tree was fast asleep till next spring. Many magical trees were sleeping and sometimes you could hear them snoring. The Oak tree was dreaming about last summer and the comings and goings of the wood. Sometimes the witch popped out of her cottage gathering winter fuel. The garden looked empty with no colourful flowers. Most of her plants went indoors for the winter. She had put some decorations outside of her cottage to brighten it up. Soon it would be Christmas. Soon there were lots of snow drops and people bring merry. The witch had lots of presents of strawberry jam and marmalade. She peered out of her window to see some blue bells and some tiny fairies buzzing around them. Soon buds began to appear on the magic rose bush and spring was around the corner. The snow had gone and the sun started to shine and the plants soon started to sprout out of the ground.

Mr fluff was changing inside his cocoon and he was dreaming of being a fairy instead of a butterfly. He had to wait all winter before he cracked open his cocoon to see what he had turned into. It was such a funny surprise for him, that he had become this orange sycamore fairy. He was such a happy soul! That it was better than being a butterfly. He soon discovered he had two tiny hands and two tiny feet. He stepped outside of his hollow and sat on the edge, trying to dry out his orange wings. Mr Fluff was a handsome little fairy, and the tree was happy to have a little friend in his hollow. Normally he got little birds nesting in it. This little thing would be a bit of a change to have a fairy!

Soon his wings were dry and he tried his best in flying into the witches garden. He saw that magic rose bush and he went to visit it. The rose bush had given him some more gold dust for his wings. So he buzzed around the witches' garden from one flower to another. To the witches surprise almost landed on her prized geraniums for a summer flower festival. "Oh look!" she said. "It is a bright orange fairy in my garden! Her mother came to look, but he was quick and vanished back over her garden wall.

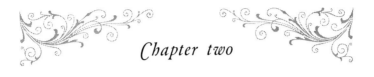

Chapter two

MR FLUFF AND HIS NEW MAGIC WAND

BY VERONICA KELLY

Mr Fluff fluttered his wings as the sun popped out of the white fluffy clouds. Some fairy dust fell in his shell and on his cosy bed. It all seemed to glow with the magic dust. A common garden snail called Brian had stopped the night in the fairies hollow and got some dust scattered on his shell. He popped his little face out to see what it was. Brian wasn't a very big snail. He was only a little snail. The fairy dust made this shell glow in the hollow. He found that the little fairy was curious about snails and told the little snail about the seashell he found on a tropical island. He also told the snail that he wanted a magic wand, because he was now ready for a bit of magic! The snail Brian couldn't speak to the little fairy. Mr Fluff didn't understand why. The little snail popped himself back inside his glowing shell. Mr Fluff didn't know how long the fairy dust would last on the common snail. The glow worms where laughing at Mr Fluff trying to talk to the snail. These magic glow worms had eaten the petals of that magic rose! The magic rose thought it would be a busy summer for magic roses. The witch Hazel sometimes collected the petals of the rose for some magic potions.

Mr Fluff flew out of his hollow wondering where he could find something to make a magic wand. So he flew to the magic rose bush to as it questions. The heads of the rose turned around to look at the fairy talking to the other roses. One rose head answered, "You will have to look deep within the forest to find something of a magical weeping willow tree that would give you something towards making your magic wand!"

"Why thank you very much" said Mr Fluff

So Mr Fluff was being naughty again! He picked a petal up and shot off in the direction of his hollow tree. He popped the petal down in front of the common garden snail. The snail was snoozing. So he tapped on his shell, and the snail woke up and popped out his head. His long snail eyes clasped eyes on the fairy that offered him something that looked very worthwhile eating. So he went to taste the magic petal. What a delightful surprise! It was the most delicious thing he had ever tasted in his snail life. He took one nibble at the beautiful leaf and soon it put a spell on him! He soon was able to talk and his very own words was, "My goodness me, that is the most gorgeous piece of grub that my little soul, has ever tasted!"

"I thought that you might have thought that! Said, Mr Fluff.

"I truly can talk to anything and anyone including that magical witch that is good to all things in her garden!"

"I'm going out to find something to make a magic wand!" said Mr Fluff.

"I wish you all the luck that you can get. Do be aware of other things in the forest other than witches and wizards. There are also things that can turn little fairy's into other things, like other creepy crawlies!" The snail was teasing the fairy. The little fairy was a bit nervous of being turned into that fat caterpillar he was once. The snail giggled at the fairy and soon scoffed the rest of that magic rose petal before any of the glow worms got a glimpse of what Mr Fluff had brought in.

The little fairy hoped that he would find his magic willow tree. Now he never talked to trees before. That Oak tree blinked an eye at a passing snail and a Robin that the little fairy who lived in his hollow, would have to talk to a lot of trees and wild plants to find his way to this magical tree. He whizzed in and out of the trees seeing all the busy bumble bees going to collect their pollen, and he saw a lot of other insects in the forest as well, He landed on a pine tree to have a rest. He felt very tired and decided to have a little nap. So he slept very well with all the buzzing insects, which came to look at a fairy having a quick snooze in the tree. It was quite something, because he had wondered so far out, that the little fairies were quite rare in this neck of the forest. Normally it was a lot of little magic folk that are called Irish Leprechauns. One was passing with his magic little pony and his belongings. He had come through a magic doorway from Ireland to England gathering magic gold and certain magic rainbows. Not many folk had seen an Irish Leprechauns in their neck of the forest. He was singing a tune with his flute. This woke up the little fairy and he heard a magic tune. He looked down below and the tree blinked its magic tree eye to see where the music was coming from. The little fairy said, "Oh" and yawned, "What a wonderful tune!"

The little man looked up and saw the pine tree wink at him. A branch pointed to words Mr Fluff in the tree. The little man had never seen a fairy like him so happy about his magic flute. Mr Fluff popped down from his resting place to look at the creature with the belongings of the little man. "Oh, what kind of creature is that?"

"That is my little pony" said the Leprechaun.

"I'm looking for a magic willow tree. That would make a suitable wand!"

"The best wands are made in Ireland Lad!"

"It would be my first wand" said the little English Fairy looking at excited.

"You need to find the magic willow tree. I can offer you a ride on my pony if you like" said the little man giggling at the fairy who really hadn't done much growing up for two summer seasons.

So the little excited fairy flew to the little pony to ride on top of the pony's fluffy mane. The little pony looked up in the air, to see this little tiny thing.

The little fairy couldn't do any magic, unless he had a wand! The little man carried on playing his flute. They travelled many nights and days. Mr Fluff was hungry little fairy. The bees had given him some nectar for dinner. It was very sweet. The little man had come with his fishing rod, and decided to have fish for supper. The little fairy wasn't interested in the little man's food, but the food the bees had given him.

The little man spotted a wild red apple tree. The tree had many flowers on its branches. There was one of two red apples hanging on its branches. He asked the little fairy to cut the stalk and drop a red apple. So the little fairy did and one rosy red apple dropped to the ground. The little man was happy, and he picked it up. He sat on a big red mushroom. He gave a small bit to the little fairy. Mr Fluff had never tasted an apple out of season before. The tree must have saved it for the magic folk that pass and travel through the magic forest. The Irish Leprechaun saved its magic seeds to plant at home. The magic apple tree was so delighted to see a little fairy. "My branches have magic, and the willow tree lives much deeper into the forest" she said, "You would have to fly on a magic moth to find it!"

She snapped a small bit if her branch and gave it to the little fairy. He kept the little magic twig. He still wanted to visit the willow tree. The little man said that he still would find it. So they travelled for more than a few days in the magic forest to find the willow tree and a magic moth showed them the way. They had travelled to find it near a river stream. There was, all the moths gathering around its trunk and all the baby caterpillars crawling up on its branches. The tree looked at the tiny little fairy and said, "You come to make a magic wand?"

"Yes" said the little fairy.

"The best bits are right into my trees branches"

The little fairy flew under the willow trees branches to find a good bit of twig. The willow tree snapped a bit of twig off and the fairy caught it well. He was such a happy fairy. Now they were happy to find their way home to Hazel and her big oak tree in her garden. The little fairy told stories about the kind witch in the forest and about her magic rose bush in her garden with all the rainbow colours in it. So they travelled back into the forest and to the cottage that Mr Fluff said he spent last winter in. There the Irish Leprechaun was invited for dinner with Mr Fluff and Hazel eating summer strawberries.

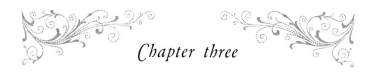

Chapter three

MR FLUFF AND THE MAGIC SEASHELL

BY VERONICA KELLY

Mr Fluff had made himself very comfortable inside the hollow of the old Oak tree. The magical branches of the tree sometimes moved about with the slight movement of the wind. The oak tree new that autumn was approaching and shed some of his leaves that turned an autumn brown. Mr Fluff looked out of his hollow, down to the ground seeing the first start of winter set in. All summer he was very busy fairy. He spent it with the caterpillars and the new fairy's that fluttered in the deep forest. They all had their favourite trees to sleep in for the autumn. Mr Fluff thought that he would sneak into the cottage with the Magic Rose bush was. He looked at his collection of leaves and he thought it wasn't enough to keep him warm in winter. Not even the silk that some magic worms had given him. The silky thread was woven into a tiny silvery blanket. Mr Fluff decided that he would pay the witch in the forest a visit for this coming autumn.

Soon it snowed so much that the little fairy popped out of his hollow and fluttered towards the cottage in the forest to see that witch called Hazel. He flew through her chimney pot before she had time to even light the logs of wood she had collected. She wondered what the little thing was, as Mr Fluff fluttered about her Lounge with some fairy magic. A little voice said, "It's me! Mr Fluff"

"It's the tiny orange fairy again!" she said. "What brings you here to my cottage?"

"It's so cold Hazel. My wings sometimes don't fly. It's cold for me to spend it in my tree" he said.

"Well if you're good you can stop the winter" Hazel said trying to light her hearth.

Mr Fluffs wings buzzed a beautiful colour like the petals of that magic rainbow rose. His little face was so sweet that he made the witch quite astonished that he had actually grown a bit since last winter. He was twice the size of a butterfly.

The witch tossed her beautiful brown locks of hair, and played with the ringlets of her hair. She had beckoned the little fairy to stand on her hand. He was quite cold to the hand. "You must stay indoors now, Mr Fluff"

"Thank you" said the little fairy.

The little fairy had made himself very comfortable in a big match box. Hazel had used all the matches in the box. So it made a good bed for him. She had put some knitted blue squares in the match box. He was quite a happy fairy. He told her that he wanted to have a beautiful seashell to sleep in the summer. That it would require a trip to a beach. Hazel was quite happy to give him a ride on her broom stick to a nice beach.

"I would like a very beautiful shell from a beach" he said.

"That would be very nice idea to dream about Mr Fluff. Now you can have some supper, and watch the snowflakes fall outside" said Hazel.

Mr Fluff fluttered out of his match box to watch the snow. On the window sill, Hazel had collected some seashells along a tropical beach. They all were so beautiful to look at. He played with them, as if he had a shell of his own. Then he fluttered his wings near the two cats. These cats belonged to the mother of Hazel. She had a black cat and a tabby long haired cat. They were sound asleep on a rocking chair. Their fur was so soft, that he fell asleep for awhile on the tabby cat. The tabby cat opened one eye to see what had landed on his fur coat. Then the cat had shut his eye again to drift and dream about what he did in the summer. He had dreamed about the fluffy white mice in the attic. Hazel had put her dolls house up there. The attic was full of dolls and toys. Some of them were musical toys that wound up. The cats went to play in it in the summer. Mr Fluff had not seen the attic yet.

Mr Fluff had spent a lovely winter with Hazel. He had enjoyed her strawberries. Soon it was time to fly to a beautiful beach on that broomstick of Hazels. This time she was ready to take him to an exotic beach. She chooses to go near the South Pacific Ocean. There were lots of other islands there. Mr Fluff went to collect his favourite shell. He picked up a brilliant green and blue shell and popped into the ruk sack of Hazel. Hazel was very busy too collecting shells on the beach. They spent a few days on the beach watching the sea come and go with the tide. It was soon time to fly back home. So Mr Fluff sat on her broom stick and soon they were off flying home.

Then they arrived home in England. Mr Fluff was very happy. He had found the perfect shell for himself to sleep in. The shell went on the window sill, with all the others. She had put some of the magic of the rose's dust inside. The shell glowed inside its own hollow. Mr Fluff went to look inside the glowing green and blue shell. "It's very roomy inside" he said.

"Would you like a blue square knitted blanket?"

"Yes, that would be very kind of you Hazel"

Soon it was summer again. Mr Fluff flew with his magic shell to put it inside the hollow of the oak tree. The little glow worms had wondered where he had gone. He told them he had been with the witch in the forest. He had gone to a faraway place to collect a magic glow shell. The little glow worms wanted to look at what he had brought back. They popped in and out of it with some excitement. The shell glowed in the dark, just like the little glow worms did. He had some lady fairies visit him and sea the magic shell. He was a very happy fairy now. The summer had just begun again. His pet dragon fly came to visit him and see Mr Fluffs new glowing shell. Sometimes you could hear mermaids singing inside the shell. He told Mr Fluff he had spent the winter with other little dragon flies. It was quite funny, because the rose bush was full in bloom again with the most beautiful roses seen for miles. It had attracted a lot of dragon flies this year, and there was a near bye pond, which had fishes in it. The dragon fly's loved it. Lots of green dragon's all showed up with the friend of the other green dragon, just to see Mr Fluffs glowing green and blue seashell. He kept flying in and out of the shell, and it started to hum a magic tune like a harp. The music sounded like the sea and singing mermaids about the depths of the big ocean. Mr Fluff said, "That must have been the witch in the cottage to make it sound like a magic singing shell. I'm so happy that it is so magical"

The clouds in the sky soon started to change. Soon there were tiny little droplets of water coming from the white fluffy clouds. Some clouds were grey and released their tiny droplets of water. "Oh!" he said, "It's going to rain!" so it did with shower of water and the seashell sung more mermaid songs of pirate ships. Mr Fluff didn't know anything about the sea, and pirate ships. The magic shell sung plenty to tell him a story about the pirates that sail vast oceans. Soon it would make him very sleepy. The rain came down, like a musical water sound outside his hollow. He put his tiny little face out to look, and the rain became much heavier. There was a small thunderstorm. He could see the witch dive out to take her washing off the line. He laughed at her with all the white sheets with rose pattern on it, getting wet. Then he looked at the rose bush and it closed all its petals. The leaves shook with the rain, and collected some of the water. The little insects disappeared under the toad stalls and the hollow of the trees in the forest. Mr Fluff had a lot of little dragons in his hollow listening to the music of the shell. Soon he fell asleep all curled up inside it.

Chapter four

MR FLUFF AND HIS MAGIC SPELL BOOK

BY VERONICA KELLY

$\mathcal{M}$r Fluff was sat on the edge of his hollow with his friend the snail who had taken a delight with eating petals from the magic rose bush. The snail was getting bigger than he ever thought he might grow. After all, he was a common garden snail, and his brown shell had changed into a rather beautiful pearly colour of soft pink and a hint of yellow. The snail normally liked to come out when raining, but today he was curled up asleep in his shell. Not a peep out of him. The magic glow worms were all sound asleep, because they liked to creep about in the dead at night. So really Mr Fluff was on his own looking out of the hollow. He had grown one inch since he had eaten that four leafed clover. He still had that golden coin to give to the Irish leprechaun when he thought the little magic man would turn up. The little man said sometimes if he had some time off he would pass this way through the woods. Mr Fluff had not seen him for some time.

The little fairy flew out of his hollow to find the witch on the topic of spell books because he needed to make his wand. He had collected two bits of magic branch and he had to find the magic ingredients for making it. So he went near the witch's garden and you could see all her prized plants. She grew a rather yellow sunflower that had a face on it. The big flower turned to look at what was buzzing around her. She opened one eye to gaze at the fluttering fairy with bright orange and yellow fluffy wings.

"My, it's a fluffy fairy!" said the flower.

"I didn't know that flowers talk?" said Mr Fluff.

"Well some magic plants do!" said the sunflower.

"Is that magic witch in her cottage?" he asked.

"She has been out shopping for stuff for her country kitchen. She has bought a lot of stuff including some spell books" said the sunflower.

Mr Fluff was excited and flew over to the window. The fluffy cat was sat their waiting to be let in. The torte shell cat meowed loudly, that the witch heard him. So she opened the window to let the cat in. Mr Fluff flew into the kitchen. It was true what the sleepy sunflower had said to him. The witch spotted that fluffy fairy again.

"Oh, I have not seen you for some time Mr Fluff" she said. "I've been buying some new wall paper and decorations for my kitchen" she said.

"I'm wondering to where I might get a spell book from?" said the little fairy.

"You would have to go into town for that!" she said. "I would have to take you into town to shop with a lot of books and maybe the shop keeper might have something special for you"

Mr Fluff grew rather excited over the thought of a spell book. He said that he had no money to pay for such a thing. So he offered his services in return for a spell book. The witch hazel was rather amused about it. So she agreed, and it would be awhile before that tiny little fairy could do any magic for her and him.

So she said that he would have to wait till tomorrow because she was so tired with all her shopping. So the little fairy decided to stay for awhile in her cottage for the rest of the hot summer afternoon. The witch had put a spell on her electric hover to hover her lounge. Mr Fluff had a ride on the handle of the machine as it whizzed around the carpet. The spell she had put on it had said the hover shouted, "All done!" Then the hover stopped. The witch sent the hover into the cupboard by another spell. The door shut the cupboard. "I can show you some spells today!" she said to the fairy. The little fairy sat down on the sofa and watched witch put a spell on the wall paper to hang on the wall. This was going to take some time sticking wall paper in the kitchen on the wall. It was rather a pretty wall paper with strawberries and red flowers on it. The spell had taken all but 3 hours to decorate the kitchen. The witch called Hazel had fallen asleep with two fluffy cats on her knee. The fairy was also taking a short nap till 8'oclock at night when he would return to his tree for the rest of the night. Hazel was truly tired out with all that flying about with the wall paper and that magic spell to stick it on the wall with sticky paste wall paper glue. Hazel's broom stick had decided to pop itself off the handle on the kitchen wall. Two glowing yellow cat's eyes in the broom looked about the lounge. The flying broom popped into the lounge and he wanted to watch the telly. The little fairy watched broom switch the telly on. This woke the witch up from her dreams. The telly was on and there was a programme about butterflies and caterpillars. Mr Fluff was excited about watching the nature programme that the witch Hazel almost forgot about what was cooking in her oven. Something meant rather nice, and she remembered there strawberry crumble."

"Oh!" she said, "I forgot about my tea!" She rushed into the kitchen to get her oven gloves on and took out her favourite crumble. Mr Fluff could smell it as well!"

"That smell rather delicious!" said the fairy.

"I quite agree" she said. It was very hot, and so she let it cool down on the kitchen work top for 20 minutes.

Mr Fluff felt very hungry and Hazel offered him a bit of crumble for his tea. He was quite happy and soon he filled his tiny little tummy with one little strawberry and some crumble with a bit of custard. This made the little fairy very full and soon he whispered that he would go to sleep in his hollow. That he would be down in the morning for the trip to the book store for his spell book.

She opened the window and the fairy had to fly on a full stomach, he managed to pop into the tree. The tree was dozing off as the sun was disappearing into the clouds. It was soon getting dark and the birds where twitting a bit. The snail was just beginning to wake up from its long snooze.

"Good evening!" said the snail, seeing the fairy yawn. The fairy was growing fast, and it was a wonder that he could fit in his magic seashell for a snooze. The snail slithered out of the entrance and out of the hollow and down the tree. He was heading straight for the rose bush, which had almost finished most of its flowering for the summer. His last chance to nibble at the fallen petals!. The snail whizzed over the witches garden wall, and was gone like a flash!

Mr Fluff slept soundly till next morning. He could hear the little birds chirping and their song that autumn would be soon coming again. Mr Fluff loved the summer and wasn't that keen about the cold winter months. He yawned and it was 7 o'clock in the morning. So he buzzed his wings for flight. He was smiling because Hazel was going to treat him to his first spell book. The orange fluffy fairy flew out of his hollow and tapped on the kitchen window. He could see the two fluffy cats waiting for their breakfast. Someone had yawned rather loudly and it was hazel. She was coming out of her bedroom into the kitchen dressed in her summer nightdress. The fairy saw her in a strawberry printed night dress. She wore some red fluffy slippers with great big yellow eyes looking up at the two hungry cats.

"Oh, it's so early!" she said to her two cats. They meowed for their bit of fish and biscuits for breakfast with a bowl of special cat milk. She soon spotted the fairy at the window tapping. So she let him in.

"How are you for a bit of breakfast then?" she said to the fairy.

"Oh, that would be nice!" he said.

So she reached her drawer and pulled a small thimble out. Then she made some tea in a teapot. She said a spell to the thimble and dipped itself into the teapot for some tea and the milk jug splashed some milk into the thimble. There was a bit of tea for the fairy. He had never seen that sort of magic before. He enjoyed his tea with some toast and jam. He was busy licking his lips with such delight in tasting the strawberry jam.

Soon the witch went into her bedroom to quickly to get dressed into some clothes. She was wearing her bright red dress and a red summer hat. She took her shiny red leather bag to and her purse. Mr Fluff knew that she was pretty well off witch and could afford to buy him just a little tiny spell book.

"Come along then!" she said to Mr Fluff.

She had fed the two cats and she was sure that Mr Fluff had a good breakfast. The little fairy popped on top of her red hat with cherry plastic bits stuck to it. He made himself very comfortable sat on her hat.

"Come along, my yellow eyed broom!" she shouted to him hanging on the wall. He soon popped down off the wall for another ride outside.

She popped onto the broom and shouted a spell to open the front door. She hovered out into the garden. Then she asked her keys by magic word to lock the door. The keys obeyed her and soon they locked the door for her. The broom was ready to fly into town. She popped her keys into her pockets. Then she said some magic words. "Fly into town, very quick, Mr Broom!"

The broom shot off into the air and high above the tree tops and the old oak tree. The broom was very fast indeed and soon had zipped in and out of the forest like a flash into a very curious magic town that sold all sorts of things. The broom soon stopped at a magic book store. The fairy had never seen anything that magic folk had. There were lots of books displayed in windows, and the shop keeper had come out to say hello to Hazel.

"Hello Hazel. Have you come to buy some more magic cookery books?"

"No, I have come to purchase a book for fairies. I have a little friend who wants to learn some simple magic!"

"Oh, fairies are quite rare treat Hazel. I have not seen one in 7 years!" the shop keeper said.

"Oh, here he is a special fairy you know, all fluffy yellow and orange!" said Hazel.

The shop keeper was quite astonished to see Mr Fluff sat on her hat, like a big fluffy moth. "Oh, I have never seen a fluffy one like that!" he said. "But I have some very small books for little children. All you need to do is cast a spell to make them smaller. The man picked a small spell book up and showed it to the fairy. It was full of spells for the garden!" It would be a good idea to learn something about making spells in the forest. So he said he was quite happy to have a spell book. She bought the spell book for the little fairy. He was quite happy. He looked at the pages and found one on how to make the wand. He had the two bits of twig he had collected. There was a spell to make the wand. He had to collect some spell bits for. She was busy with her special fairy's collecting musical boxes for her kingdom.

Mr Fluff and Hazel soon left the shop of magic spell books. Hazel had bought some magic cookery spell books for making magical fairy big cakes. So she could make some for her friends and herself. The witches broom went flying back home because the witch wanted to show the little fairy some of her magic on dainty cakes. Hazel loved cooking and making cakes of all descriptions. It was not to long before the witch got home and found the two cats meowing. They were hungry and she had realised that she had been flying out of all morning on her broomstick. That the broom stick was tired too and wanted to go off for a quick nap back on the wall he usually slept in the kitchen. The little fairy flew near the sofa and sat on the arms rest and decided he could have a little nap. The fluffy torte shell cat purred at the fluffy yellow and orange fairy. The fairy jumped on the back of the cat. The fairy and the cat seemed to enjoy each other's company. The cat was a bit playful with the fairy. So the fairy flew about the lounge and landed on the magic cookery books that Hazel had bought. He soon yawned a bit, and the eyes of the books winked a Hazel. The little fairy fell asleep on the magic cookery book for fairy cakes!

Chapter five

MR FLUFF AND THE RAINBOW QUEEN

BY VERONICA KELLY

One summer morning, the sun had just vanished behind the silver grey clouds above a magic forest. The rain started to drop in tiny droplets and it sounded like musical notes. Mr Fluff had yawned and popped out of his sleepy hollow to see what the weather was like. "Oh, it's raining!" He said to the tree. The tree said, "It's very good for me. I'm quite thirsty these days and my roots grow quite deep in the ground. Mr Fluff flew to the top of the tree and saw a big rainbow. He was very excited. It was told by the tree, that a magic Rainbow fairy lived there. So he thought he would go on an adventure to find her. Mr Fluff spread his wings, and he knew he would get a bit wet in the rain. He said to the tree that he was off to visit this rainbow queen. He had heard some tales about a beautiful fairy that lived near a big

31

magical rainbow past the deep forest. The tree smiled, and off the little fairy flew over the tops of the trees and in and out of the ever winding trees. He could hear the sound of the forest, and twittering of the birds, and the bees rush around the trees and dive for cover under the huge trees. The water droplets where quite big, and they splashed heavily to the ground and bounced around the leaves. Mr Fluff was getting a bit wet and his wings were getting wet too. He hoped he had enough fairy dust on him that the magic rose bush that carefully dusted his wings. He kept smiling though, and he saw many magic folk singing songs in the rain.

Mr Fluff found himself a nice red toadstool to shelter out of the rain. A Big lady bird had found another toadstool near bye and she had a troop of baby lady birds all following her. Mr Fluff had never seen such little things. He was growing just a bit. He was bigger than the average caterpillar. In fact that he had grown twice as long as the average moth caterpillar he should have been.

"Oh I am getting wet!" said Mr Fluff to the lady Bird.

"Soon it will be all over with the rain!" she said.

"It seems to go on forever. Mrs Ladybird" he looked very wet and sorry for himself. There was a tiny bit of sun just peering through the clouds and a huge rainbow appeared!

Funny enough in this deep forest there was many pieces of magic that consisted of certain types of roses! In the deep forest floor was another rainbow rose that had been planted by magic tiny folk. "Oh look at the most delicious rainbow petals my eyes have ever seen!" he could see the young rose bush and it had rather a lot of bees collecting pollen from it and some of the rose heads had made seeds already. So Mr Fluff had collected one seed head to take back home with him. He wanted to grow something in a pot in his tree. It would be nice to have some magic baby rose bush in his hollow. There was another very old magic rose bush that was moved to the old cottage garden before Hazel and her mother Lillian had decided to buy the cottage and the barn. It was put there in its last bit of life because when these roses' bushes die they release enormous amount of magic energy that looks like fireworks when it goes off. It in fact is quite potent stuff to handle as the rose turns into a lot of fairy glittery dust powder. It is used in very strong wizard and witch magic for some potent bazaar spells for bringing things back to life and changing things that are ordinary into extraordinary if you like.

"Well someone called hazel had brought a cottage at the edge of the forest and the mother had wanted to purchase the land to a very old barn with a magical port door. This was the door to another world of ghosts. There were usually the other fairy goblin folk that used it when they died to live their last part of their magical existence in such a place. Naturally there were other port doors and mirrors about for such as Lillian and her aunt Claudia to use when they departed. Claudia was departed and had not yet made any form of seeing what her niece was up to. In fact that Claudia her wicked aunt had gone through her own rose mirror that was now packed in a box with a load of soft packaging. Claudia could only see through the other end with all the pink packaging. That meant her niece was in the process of unpacking stuff from the big mansion house and at present could not spy on her living niece and Hazel.

It was not long before he felt some magic touch him, by a very strange rainbow woman within the heart of the rose bush itself. A warm breeze drying his wings in the form of a ladies hand wafted around him. He fluttered his wings about and then spotted some four leaf clover growing and had some of the leaves to eat. His wings did beat faster like that of a bumble bee. He ate the clover and felt the magic and made him grow a bit bigger than he thought. The magic was doing its job. He had grown a extra inch taller than last month since he hatched over the two summers.

There was an Irish Leprechaun sat on a red and white spotted toad stall. He was eating his lunch and he managed to see the tiny fairy flutter his wings and he was now about 3 inches and a bit tall. "There's lots of magic in these woods little orange fairy!" If you fly about over that rainbow you would meet that rainbow fairy!" said the Leprechaun.

Mr Fluff buzzed off with some excitement to the rather coloured rainbow to see a big huge tub of gold at the end and rather a lot of Leprechauns gaze at the magic and collected it in their leather purses. Their sat on one of the pink and purple roses was the rainbow fairy with a lot of colours in her wings. She had golden hair as long as a pony's mane. She was blowing out magic bubbles in the forest. Some of them drifted off like big round coloured light balls. One popped near Mr Fluff and the tiny bubble released some coloured dust on his wings that made them shimmer. The fairy looked like a young girl of sixteen with fluttering wings. She spotted Mr Fluff popping the bubbles and playing with them. "Oh, a very bright orange fairy playing with my bubbles!" she said.

The rainbow fairy queen who was only young had wings that glittered so much like a purple emperor and she was six inches tall. She wanted to play with the orange fairy and sat Mr Fluff on her knee for a short time. He was very much like a very small little boy that liked to play with things! She told him he would be a very special orange fairy one day and he would do lots of magic. So to say that this forest was under a very dangerous thousand year spell. No one knew how long they would last and things without anyone knowing how to do such powerful witching magic could actually save it. It had to be done by a green witch with a special gift. They had to crack the spell to end the one that it had. The leprechauns had read all about it in one of their magic newspaper articles that the forest could vanish forever if they did not find such a powerful witch to brew such magic and find the codex book that their world would not be gone forever. These Leprechauns where gathering up the last bits of magic in the forest. They said that the fairies would die and it would be a sad thing! There muttering was heard with their magic keys to the doorway of their world. One of their magic crystal balls said there would be such a witch that could perform a powerful spell. This made them look at Isaacs green crystal ball and they could see a cottage on the edge of the forest with two witches inside it. They all stopped to look at each other. They would have to arrange to pay these two witches a flying visit. There could be Leprechaun gold paid for if she dared do it, said one of the little men. This made the orange fairy suddenly startle and cry if there was no magic and we would vanish in a puff of smoke. There was a black troll hiding deep in the forest doing bad spells on things he was part of the bad omen and he was after the codex book and its magic!

The rainbow fairy said that she heard of a witch called Lillian that had come from Derby to live in one of their forests. She is to have old magic. "I wouldn't worry about things like dying" said the rainbow queen. "We fairies have long acquaintances with witches from all over Derbyshire and their full of sort of potent magic that is said that a green witch that was born from a green dragons egg would break the spell"

There was plenty of time left to go chasing after a codex book and to get rid of a bad Troll that was doing bad things. There was a few years left at least. The little fairy had stopping sobbing about everything coming to an end! But the goblins and the Irish Leprechaun had gone on wilting for a good hour and half about the whole forest disappearing in one deadly black spell. One leprechaun named Isaac said, "You can have a gold coin!" So it was tiny coin from rather a big bushel of coins found appearing at the end of a big rainbow. "Be careful how you spend your money little man!" said the Leprechaun. So off he flew with one of the other fairies back to his tiny hollow. She came to see where Mr Fluff had his home!

"How very small!" she said. Suddenly she fluttered and waved her wand on the tree and made the hollow much bigger. This was much better for the little orange fairy. "Still got some magic left" she said disappearing into the forest.

There were voices coming from the cottage. It was Lillian who had peered into the crystal ball seeing very dark figure and a horrible demon red and yellow eyes staring back at her and the sound of his voice almost broke her crystal pink ball. She flung a dish cloth over it and hoped what-ever she saw would vanish. But the cottage and its soul trembled in its presence. The two cats being a bit magic had poked one of their paws at the beast! There was a scuffle and then one of the cats with big green eyes said, "The one who has the other codex book has the deadliest spell of all" In fact there was two codex books and one of them is in a huge library for Goblins and Leprechauns and the other was missing and not found.

"Oh goodness!", said Lillian and Hazel. "My two cats have never talked before!"

"You never thought that we cats have magic too!" said the black cat. The cat began to purr. "I hope you have a good wand!" the cat said curling into a ball on the rocking chair.

"I've seen an orange fairy!" blinked the other cat.

"Yes, I do believe we have a lodger in our garden!" said Hazel

"There is much to do with magic in this neck of the woods" said Lillian. She thought what she saw in her precious pink crystal ball of such dark magic.

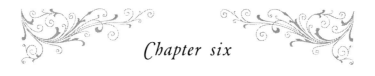

Chapter six

MR FLUFF AND HIS MAGICAL GEM STONE

BY VERONICA KELLY

Mr Fluff had woken up in his Oak tree and the Oak tree said it would soon become autumn. "I'm going to sleep for a long time through the winter months" said the tree, to the little orange and yellow fairy. The tree had started to turn its leaves a golden brown and some of them fell to the ground. Mr Fluff was looking through his new spell book that the witch had bought him. He wanted a nice cosy warm hollow. This time he was not using oak leaves to fill his cosy home with. He sat down thinking what kind of spell to use to make his hollow nice and warm. The glow worms liked the dampness of the hollow and said that they would have to find another home if he made it so warm. The tree said, "Look here, I have another hollow a bit higher up in my trunk. So when the time comes you can wriggle up there and the fairy will have to learn his new bit if magic!"

"How many hollow holes have you got then?" asked Mr Fluff.

"I think I have about three" said the tree.

"What's inside them?"

"Little caterpillars!" giggled the tree. "They would become butterflies"

"No birds then?" said the fairy.

"No birds" shrugged the tree.

Mr Fluff looked through all the pages for a cosy warm hollow and found a spell to enchant the hollow to make it warmer. He had to collect a magic glow stone from a crystal merchant. He wondered how he would meet such a person to get him a glow stone. Well he didn't have long to wait because the Irish Leprechaun had come with his talking pony. He was playing his flute again, and Mr Fluff shot out of the hollow as fast as a bumble bee. He shouted out aloud at the little man. The little man looked up to see his little orange friend

"Hello!" said the fairy. "I wonder if you can help me get a magic glow stone from."

"Oh, there's always a bit of travelling to do with magic gem stones!" said the Irish Leprechaun. "What type and colour of stone, would you have in mind?"

"Oh, a pretty stone" said the fairy.

"That would take you to the edge of the forest for a gold coin then!"

"I have a gold coin that the Leprechaun gave me awhile ago" said the fairy.

So Mr Fluff had buzzed in his hollow to get the gold coin and give it to the Irish Leprechaun. The little man bit the coin to see whether it was fairy gold. True enough it was. So the fairy would have to travel into the forest to see a man about magic gem stone.

They travelled deep into the forest with the little white pony and the little man. There was a light shining from a very big chestnut tree. It was the biggest tree that the little fairy had seen. The little Leprechaun said it were the man with the gem stones lived. I would be too far to travel into town to go and get one. The Leprechaun tapped on the big door and a little man popped his head around the door. A voice said, "Come in!" and the door creaked open for them. It was an odd sort of place with dozens of mugs hanging on the wall of this big hollow. There were pictures on the walls and gem stones on a ledge near the fire place. This old tree had been dead for a long time. The little man with the gem stones made some tea on a stove. He said that he had lived in the tree for a long time. He was surprised to see an orange and yellow fairy looking at his collection of mugs on the wall.

"What kind of stone were you looking for my fluffy friend?"

The fairy didn't know anything about what stone he had in mind. "One that you can enchant" he said with a smile.

"What kind of enchantments are you going to do?" asked the man looking at his precious stones. "Most of these are very expensive. You can have this green stone called Malachite"

"It's a very pretty stone isn't it?" Mr Fluff, the little fairy said picking it up. The stone was fairly small for the little fairy to pick up. This meant it was the right size for him to take home. "Yes I will have that green stone and enchant it in my hollow to keep it warm this winter.

The little man gave the stone to the fairy and he popped in his small hands. He soon would have to make himself a bag to carry it. The little man opened a jewel box and inside was a small leather purse. It was empty and just the right size for the stone to be put in. So he gave it to the little fairy and the little tiny thing fluttered his wings with excitement. The man said "You better be on your way home soon!"

"Yes it is getting dark soon" said the Leprechaun.

"That magic stone is for travellers" said the gem stone. "Do you fly a lot about the forest?" asked the little man.

"I do a lot of flying everywhere especially in the summer" said the little fairy.

The leprechaun wanted something else for the gold. That was a rather large moonstone. He could have it made into a ring. He also wanted some exotic tea from India so it would last some winter months. He told the little fairy he loved drinking tea and having lots of cakes with all different colours of decorations on it. He had a soft tooth for cakes. Mr Fluff had never eaten any sort of cake. The witch he knew loved her strawberries and she would be busy making pots of red jam for her winter months.

"Let's go then, it's almost getting dark and soon the clocks go back and soon it will be Halloween so that's when a lot of witches will be flying about on their broom sticks!" said the Leprechaun.

They left the man in his tree and outside you could see smoke coming out of the chimney. The old tree was turned into a tree house. Outside were lots of fire flies buzzing around the old dead tree.

They were soon off and the little white pony trotted off into the woods and the journey took almost three hours to arrive home. Mr Fluff was very tired and the Oak tree peeped open one eye to see something orange and fluffy buzz into one of his hollows. The old tree saw the white pony and the leprechaun going off into the direction of a magic garden with a gate. That gate was painted a bright emerald green with lots of vines growing around it. The little man and his pony opened the gate with an enchanted spell. Then the gate opened and they seemed to disappear when they passed through to the secret garden and a magical flash of light appeared, and they were gone!

Mr Fluff was yawning wide and put the leather bag down near his shell. He popped into his cosy shell to here the song of the sea. He had thoughts about having a musical box, but that would have to wait awhile. He was in his little fairy bed and he wanted to gaze at the fairy green stone. He pulled it out of the leather sack and then looked at his spell book. Maybe tomorrow he would have a go at enchanting the stone to glow. So the little fairy soon fell asleep, and so did the tree and you could hear the tree sometimes snoring.

The pink pearly snail popped back through the hollow to find his friend the fairy fast asleep. The snail had the last of the magic rose's petals and the plant had put a spell on the snail. The snail was wondering what kind of spell the rose bush has bestowed upon him. This was probably a growing spell. It was rather a funny spell that the rose bush does with most creatures that nibble away at its rose bushes and petals. The snail was rather full as well and he could feel himself growing double in size! "What will that little fairy think!" said the snail and tucked himself inside his new gorgeous pink pearly shell.

The next morning Mr Fluff was having a bit of a go at casting a spell to enchant the green stone to glow. He had two bits of magic stick. It was rather funny to see this fairy about with two bits of stick that really hadn't been turned into a wand at all. He was waving the twig about and lot of dust lit and popped out the end of the magic stick of the willow tree. It certainly made his hollow warm, but the spells were not that easy for a beginner. A voice warned him not to set the tree alight with wrong sort of magic!

"I'm trying my best to enchant the stone!" said the fairy.

"Dust light isn't a good idea!" warned the tree.

"I must visit the witch again, and maybe she could make me a wand!"

"That sounds a good idea!" said the oak tree.

So the little fairy flew out of the tree and buzzed on the window of the kitchen. Hazel was making some red strawberry jam. You could see her magic inside the window, and things were moving about on the stove. You could almost smell the jam from the gaps in the window frame. He knocked hard on the window, and her pet cat with the great big green eyes let him in. He was a big fluffy black cat. The other torte-shell had fallen fast asleep on the rocking chair. The black cat meowed loudly to say that she had a fluffy visitor and it's all about a magic wand. The witch stopped in the middle of her spell to look at her talking black cat. A fairy was sat on the fluffy black cat.

"What seems to be the problem?" she asked the fairy who was a bit frustrated.

"I need to make my magic wand work" he said, "All I can do is making light dust glow in my hollow"

"Oh dear!" said the witch. "You'll have to give me the bits of stuff for the wand I will have to put a spell on them. So you'll have to give them to me"

So he rushed out of the window and collected his two bits of magic twig and gave them to the witch. So she made a special spell to weave to bits together and put a tiny sequin star on the end of it. She had lots of sequins in her knitting box at the bottom. So putting a green one on the end made it rather pretty for him. Then she told the wand another magic spell. So it could only be used by the magic orange fairy. So he was delighted and fluttered off back home to boast to the oak tree that he had a proper wand!

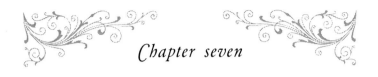

Chapter seven

MR FLUFF AND HIS MAGIC GREEN FAIRY CAKES

BY VERONICA KELLY

$\mathcal{M}$r Fluff was reading his magic spell book that the nice witch Hazel had bought him earlier in the summer. It was the late evening and the nights had already begun to draw in. He had found a nice spell on fairy cakes and the liked the one about the green fairy cake with all the glittery sparkly icing decorations on it. He would have to collect some potions for the spell and so he made a list of them in his green note book that he had conjured by magic with his wand. The list was ingredients for a basic recipe of lightly baked sponge cakes. On his list was white sugar. So he wrote it down in his green note book. Then he would have to get some self raising flour for baking. So he wrote that down. Then he needed some green minty mixture from an herb plant. It seemed that the witch had some in her garden! So off he flew to pull a few leaves off before he could be seen. Then he quickly disappeared over her garden wall. Then there was the soft margarine to get. So he had to get that from somewhere. So he used another magic spell to conjure a bowl full of soft margarine. You know where that bowl of margarine had come from! A woman in a cake store had just put down a small bowl with margarine in it, and suddenly with fairy magic from nowhere, the bowl vanished in a bright ray of glittery star dust! So Mr Fluff hadn't any idea what the wand had done. So he did the same for the flour and he did for the sugar and they all came from different cake shops! The little fairy began to mix all the ingredients together and also an egg from a chicken. Then he added the mint leaves and did a green spell with it. So it was very green indeed. He added some fairy green dust and then with his wand he wavered it about to put the contents in a conjured baking tray for a big cake. He had a lot of mixture left so he conjured some green doilies to make small fairy cakes. Then waved his wand about and suddenly they cooked! He had also put some green coloured decorations on the big cake and the small cake. He was very pleased with himself. He decided to eat one of this fairy cakes. It was very spongy and minty and the decorations tasted very scrumptious.

"That looks interesting?" said Brian the pink snail looking at the green fairy cakes. So the little fairy gave the pink snail a green cake. The snail had really found himself a treat.

"You've been cooking some nice green cakes!" said the old Oak tree.

"Yes, I have and I suppose you can taste one of them as well" said the little orange fairy that was still eating his share of the cakes.

"That would be very nice of you" said the tree with his glowing green eyes and a big smile. So the tree moved his branches out waiting for the fairy to give him a fairy green cake.

"Here you are!" said the fairy, as he flew out of the hollow and found a moving branch that wanted the green cake. So the tree the green cake went down whole in the mouth of the magic tree. The funny thing was the green cake had made the tree produce green sparkly glitter all over the branches that had just shed a big pile of autumn orange leaves. The cake was very minty and the tree wanted another cake. So he asked for a second cake. The fairy allowed him to have another cake and the same thing happened again with all the green fairy dust!

"I'm off to deliver the big fairy cake to the witch in her cottage" said the little fairy. He made another flying spell so the green sparkly cake hovered out of the hollow and magically through the bark of the tree. Mr Fluff had made a very big green cake so it really would not fit through his hollow. So the magic had transported it outside. He followed the hovering cake that went over the garden wall and then hovered her kitchen window.

"Hello!" shouted the little orange fairy and tapped on the kitchen window. The black cat saw the funny little orange fairy wanting to be let in. The black cat with the green eyes knew that his mistress was sound asleep on her rocking chair with cookery book clasped to her right hand. The black cat went to ask her broom stick to open the kitchen back door. The broom stick hopped off the handle he was hanging on and magically made his way to the kitchen back door and a spell to open it. The door opened up and a cake came wafting into the kitchen which was accompanied by an orange fairy. The fairy decided to leave it on the kitchen work top and he buzzed around the witch and scattered some green fairy dust all over her. Her nose twitched and the young witch Hazel woke up. She could see her mother's black cat called midnight purring and looking at the green cake.

"Well its Mr Fluff isn't it again. How are we doing then?" she asked.

"I promised that I would give you something in return for the spell book. So I decided to make you a big green fairy cake. I made it myself this morning. The tree and the snail have had some little green cakes!"

"What a wonderful surprise to have you do me a nice green fairy cake!" she said thinking what kind of magic would do if she tasted it. So she looked into her green crystal ball in her living room. A face appeared inside the ball of a green goblin. "There's no harm of the fairy cake!" the little goblin vanished as he quickly appeared. So she tasted the green fairy cake and made herself a pot of tea with some magic and the little fairy enjoyed himself. He was also trying make his own tea spell out of one of the witches tea books. The black cat nibbled at a piece of fairy cake. He meowed so loudly, and the funny thing was the green fairy dust scattered all over his black silky fur and he truly sparkled. He went meow! "Wouldn't this look good on Halloween!" he purred.

Mr Fluff saw a bit of sparkly green dust scatter on the witch and she giggled as she ate more of the fairy cake. She found herself floating up to the ceiling and then back down again.

Mr Fluff went back to his hollow and offered more green cakes for the tree. The tree had a few more of his green cakes and lots of sparkly green glitter scattered all over the tree again. Mr Fluff saved the rest of the green cakes for the rest of the week. He had to think what other kind of spell he could do making more green fairy puddings! The sun went down and disappeared and the little fairy fell asleep in his musical shell listening to the sound of singing voices of distant mermaids. He was soon fast asleep dreaming that he was on a nice golden beach with lots of beautiful mermaids sitting on the rocks singing about boats and fish. Sometimes the mermaid song sounded like dolphins singing and sometimes a sound like a watery harp. He said the mermaids in a dream that he must make sweet green apple crumble by a magic spell! But he tried and something bazaar happened! He got a lot of sea weed turn up on his dinner plate! Plus a crab scuttle across his wooden table.

Mr Fluff woke up again he go out his spell book and began to flick through the pages for a green apple. Then he rememebered that there was a red apple tree in the forest not far from the kind witches cottage. Mr Fluff had seen her fly her broom stick for the red apples and wondered it was a good idea to have some of his own. So off he went into the forest looking for the red apple tree. He eventually found her fast asleep an he picked at one of the red apples and it fell to the ground with such a bump. The tree had woken up to see a giggling fairy up to mischief.

"You're pinching my apples!" she said.

"Oh my goodness, another talking tree!" remarked the fairy.

"Why it isn't many fairie's that come this way only the witch near that magic rose bush!"

"I would like some apples. Maybe three rosie red apples because I want to make a crumble" he said.

"Oh, ok then. What will be the pleasure of your name orange fairy?"

"My name is Mr Fluff and I live in that old Oak tree near the witches cottage"

"The old Oak tree is very far from here. You must have flown a long way then?" she said.

"Yes" and so he made a hovering spell for the roseie red apples to follow him home to his tree. The red apple tree giggled at his magic, because he was a beginner and sometimes the apples pulled faces at him and they bounced on the ground like a ball. He had to keep making his magic spell to keep the apples flying in the air. It was getting towords mid morning when he arrived home rather tired with three apples with giggling faces laughing at him.

The red apple trees magic apples where to magical for him and they found a opportunity that they would escape his magic and they bounced out of the hollow and over the witches garden. She was fast asleep and dreaming of other nice things. The apples vanished indoors to look at two cats licking their paws. The little fairy went to find his magic apples in the witches kitchen giggling so loudly that the witch woke up.

"Oh some magic apples!" she said. "You must have been far away in the forest Mr Fluff. Those are not cooking apples dear!"

"I wanted to make an apple crumble!" he said almost in tears.

"Those are magic apples for goblins and that friend of yours. We will save them for that magic pony of his when he visits in the autumn. He always comes to buy different types of tea. As I buy all sorts of brands of tea that you can drink!"

"So have you got any tea on offer for me?"

"How about an English breakfast tea!" she said making a spell for the cupboard and the teapot. She watched the copper kettle boil on the cooker and the kettle pour hot water in the laughing teapot.

Mr Fluff was learning about that magic forest he was living in. All things in their ways have different types of magic! So Mr Fluff has a lot of spells and magic to learn. He keeps that witch laughing as he practices in his hollow place in the tree.

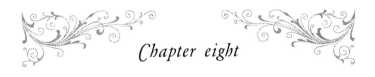

Chapter eight

MR FLUFF AND HIS NEW MAGIC HOLLOW DOOR

BY VERONICA KELLY

The little orange fairy was thinking how cold it was last winter. He had wanted to keep warm inside his tiny little hollow. The Gem stone needed a magic spell to keep him warm like a hot water bottle. The witch went to sleep with one. Last winter she had a red water bottle and pump attached to the device. She had knitted the water bottle a red cover and put the cover on it. She mentioned Christmas at the end of the year. As a fairy he really didn't understand anything about it. He watched her send lots of cards to her friends and one to the shop keeper with the magic spell books.

He decides that he wanted to ask the tree before the idea of putting a magic hollow door on one of his hollows. Well that sane evening when autumn leaves began to fall and the tree snoring their heads off. The little fairy tapped on his bark at the base of the tree.

"My goodness . . . . it's that tiny fairy!"

"I wondered if you could allow me to get hold of a magic hollow door?" the fairy piped with a tiny smile.

"Yes, I think that's a good idea for you. I think its going to be very white snowy winter if you ask me!" The tree smiled at the fairy getting very excited of the idea of a magic door.

Off the fairy went into the woods to see that magical witch Hazel that he wanted to buy a magic door. She agreed to take him shopping on her broom stick to a store who sold such things to tiny folk!

Hazel flew into the woods and high over the trees and it was such a long way into town. She flew in out of the streets to find a woodman who carved things for small folk like the fairy she had on her red hat.

He was sat outside carving a magic door another fairy that came into town with a wizard. The wizard said to the witch he had a pet fairy who liked to play in his garden with all the giant pumpkins he grew for the children to make lanterns.

The witch Hazel said that her fairy was found in the oak tree where she lived on the edge of the forest. The little orange fairy looked at the white fairy with some interest. The Wizard said, "White fairies are very rare! Though sometimes when it snows, she puts a magic spell on the snow that has fallen on the trees and the trees glow with a silvery glint at night"

The witch Hazel smiled at the tiny little female white fairy. "My fairy is learning his magic!" He likes to make all sorts of coloured fairy cakes. I have brought him to town to get a fairy hollow door"

Inside the shop there was a warm glowing fire and a huge big dresser that had lots of magic opening doors for all sorts of small people. Mr Fluff decided to have a good look at all the doors. They came in all shapes and sizes and he buzzed around them like a bumble bee. He waved his tiny little hands opening and shutting the doors. He had little magic hands to open the doors and he liked the bright fluorescent door handle on the carved wooden ivy. He said that this door was in the one for him.

The witch had to buy him the door and seemed that he would have to do her some fairy magic in return. She paid the man some money and went to another shop to buy some treats for her two cats. The magic hollow door had a door chime fitted to it.

The little fairy started to play with all the door chimes in the shop. He liked the door chime that sounded like magical playing harp. "Oh this one!" he said that would do for his door bell.

The witch said "Oh! That would surely break the bank!"

Mr Fluff didn't mean to embarrass the witch. Not knowing how much the door bell cost. That she just had enough money to pay for it. Other than, her pets food items that she had to buy at the pet shop. The wizard in the purple hat chuckled at the funny orange fairy. The white fairy tried to whisper in his ear that some things cost a lot of money! He said he was very sorry and didn't understand much about money. That he hadn't any himself to pay for the door. The witch in the red hat had found it all funny about the whole thing! She had a good sum of money left in a will by her Great Uncle Sebastian. So she thought about it because she purchased the cottage and her mother had bought the barn and the land that went with it. Her mother had an idea in her head for a lodge sort of place to build something like a house made of wood. The cottage was purchased on discounted offer, because it had not been lived in for 200 years. It was cited in a very remote place of the forest. Where to her there are a lot of secret things in the forest. There are magical doorways that included something that the little fairy hadn't even got a clued about. So she hummed and said, "Well its isn't it and I think the tree would be pleased to have something sound like a musical harp playing now and again!"

"Oh, so that's in agreement of 25 pieces of special coinage with the green leafed clover on the front of the coin" said the shop keeper.

Well he soon got a box to put the fairy door in and the magical harp chime. The little fairy had no idea that this young friendly Witch was splashing a bit out on her friends with her money she had from an uncle.

The white fairy buzzed around the shop keepers magical doors playing all the different door chimes. Mr Fluff sat one top of one magic door with his orange wings buzzing. He was wondering how people made money. So they would go out and spend it. The Witch would have to explain to him that people go out and work in different jobs and are paid money. She had known of the fairy for 3 years and he was still a youngster learning his magic cooking skills!

"Thanks very much I'll be on my way to shop to get some stuff for my two cats!" said the witch.

"Thanks very much I'll be on my way to the shop to get some stuff for my two cats!" said the witch.

The orange fairy jumped off a magic door with a face on it. As he looked at the door winked at him! So the little fairy flew into the bright red witch's hat for a cosy ride while she buzzed around on her broom stick to the next shop.

It wasn't too far for the broom to remember where the pet shop was and the door opened to let them in. She gave the shop keeper a piece of paper with a list of fish for the cat's supper. There were 14 tins of different types of fish for cats to enjoy and the cost 10 special coins with green leafed clover on it. She was loading up the broom stick with all the shopping. She still had to do her own!

"Oh, shall have to fly back home!" she said, "With two big boxes. That I would have to do my ingredient shopping another day!" she said to the fairy. "Oh, I'm quite tired with all this flying on my broom" She yawned.

That was quite funny, because the little orange fairy had fallen fast asleep in her red pointed hat. The broom winked at the witch when she yawned again. Off he took, and they were high above the clouds looking like a big puff balls of white candy floss. The magic forest wasn't too far away and soon the broom lowered itself and darted in and out of the swaying trees. Some of the trees chattered amongst themselves. If you were silent enough, you were silent enough, you could hear the tiny voices of the tiny fairies that did their magic by night fall. The witch was very sleepy and just about could steady herself on her broom. The broom stopped and it was getting very dark and the only things that glowed was the glow worms in the trees, and one swift buzzing and 20 or so fairies whizzed past her broom and they all twinkled in different coloured lights. Their chatter disappeared into the forest.

The witch fiddled in her shopping bag for a torch! Because it was so dark, that flying at night time was so difficult. So she put her torch light on, and her broom flew steady in and out of the trees. You could see in a distance that her cottage was lit with reddish yellow glow!

Not a peep out of Mr Fluff, because he was so tired he was dreaming about his supper before going to bed. It wasn't long before she arrived home and her magic big door opened up as they flew in. She parked her broom in the kitchen and put the boxes on the kitchen table. She took off her hat, and warmed herself buy the fire. It's a good thing she had her mother fast asleep in a rocking chair to keep the house warm. That she was stopping over the winter time and helping out with the decorations of the other rooms in the cottage. Lots of spells, so Mr Fluff was only a little thing to help with some magic! That now and again he needed his summer hollow to have a nice front door on it. She would fit the door later with a pair of ladders. She would have to have the spell instruction for the attachment of the door. She let him sleep all cosy in her red hat. She went over to her larder to have some mince pies and some tea before dozing off herself.

Something smelt the smell of cakes and Mr Fluff wanted a piece of cake and his supper. Hazel was surprised at the tiny fairy waking up! He was very hungry and eats some cake. He loved the Earl grey tea she had bought and she had many types of tea in her larder store. She had a very big tea pot and the brass kettle was boiling over the old stove. Her mother said that you need a new kitchen fitted soon. Last summer she had only walk papered the walls. "Oh that's more spending money!" she said. I would have to earn some money with my recipe cookery spell books!"

The fairy had his supper and said to the witch, "Oh, its, to cold! Can I sleep in your cottage tonight? He asked.

"Yes, I think it's going to snow soon!" she said. "Have a good night"

He slept soundly into the next morning. To be awakened with the two cats wanting their breakfast. Hazel was down stairs singing to herself and opened the box with the hollow door for the fairy. The musical door played the harp for her and awoke the fairy that slept with the fluffy black. The airy went to see his hollow door and asked when she would put it up soon.

"Oh I shall have to get to my ladders out and my spell book to fix in your oak tree" she said. "Let's have breakfast"

The little fairy had breakfast of some muffins and some English Tea. Then later the witch went to get her ladders and went into the garden. The very next thing that she did, was the magic spell for the hollow door! The little fairy watched the witch make a spell to fit it to the hollow. This woke the sleeping Oak tree up to be so surprised. He looked up at Hazel and the door making all the sounds of a musical harp.

"That should do us a treat in the winter. It is cold enough to snow! I saw that little white fairy last night!" said the tree giggling at the other fairy.

"I guess that's funny then, where in for a bit of snow!" said the witch.

"It's too cold for me to sleep in there!" he said. "I need my magic stone and my shell to be brought indoors!" said the little fairy to the witch half way up the ladder.

"All in good time Mr Fluff! I grab your shell and stone then" so she did with her hand and put it in her leather bag. She soon came down the ladder and you know what!" Tiny flakes of snow began to fall in the forest. Mr Fluff was so excited about it, that the white fairy would be visiting him over the winter snow. Mr Fluff looked up at the sky. It was so grey and white without any clouds that the snowflakes became thicker and the witch rushed indoors with her ladders and his possessions and the orange fairy flew through the cat flap.

"Oh it's cold out there!" she said "Come and warm yourself up"

The tree outside was pleased to hear some tunes that the door made, and so was the tiny glow worms. The pink snail popped out of his shell to see what the witch had done!" Then he popped himself back into the shell for a long winter snooze. It was still cold in the hollow though. Mr Fluff hadn't learnt enough to keep his hollow warm yet.

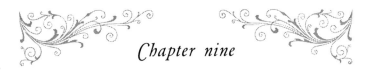

Chapter nine

MR FLUFF AND HIS MUSICAL MAGIC BOX

BY VERONICA KELLY

One day when it was snowing he was sat beside a big tree with coloured lights all twinkling brightly. Hazel was buzzing around busy unwrapping presents for her mother and some other friends. Mr Fluff had no idea that it was soon Christmas day. He was playing with the coloured baubles that the Witch had put on the tree and she said to him, "You know it is also winter solstice and people give each other presents as well!"

The fairy liked the bright red orange baubles that hazel had put up including all the glittery tinsel and made a twinkle bit around his waist. He was laughing at himself and saw his reflection inside a silver bauble. The mother of Hazel said to the fairy, "They cast your reflection, and so you should make a wish!"

The little fairy wanted musical things and so he whispered for a musical playing magical box. So sometimes he wanted to sleep in it. It would be very good idea for him to play the musical box.

There were a lot of Christmas cards and winter solstice cards all over the wall were the Witch had pinned them up. He went to look at them all and saw that the Wizard had sent her winter solstice card with a white fairy on it. Hazel said that people gave each other presents and Mr Fluff hadn't any money for this sort of event. He was too happy to play with the baubles with the black fluffy pussy cat that allowed him to sleep with her at night time. She was in a playful mood and played with a bauble around the lounge and meowed at the fairy to join in. Mr Fluff was trying out his magic wand on some of the green baubles and sometimes you could see something reflect inside them. He could see magical boxes all playing different tunes and then mince tarts on a red clothed table. "They look good" and he tried a magical spell he had learnt yesterday for mince pies. It was a surprise he had made for some magic for red tarts instead of mice tarts and they were so small! That he ate all four of the jam tarts for himself and soon fell asleep on one of the baubles on the tree. He was asleep for a long time. "Come and look at the window, it has snowed in my garden!"

So the little fairy looked outside to see the snow cover her garden and the wall. The big oak tree was wide awake looking at some little robins and Hazel had put some bird food for them. The tree swayed its branches to knock of the snow. Then he yawned and the magic hollow door started to play a tune. The tiny pink snail popped out his sleepy head, and out of the door. "Oh my goodness it's all snow!" Then shut the door and felt as if he could eat a few green leafs that he gathered up one cold no night from magic ivy so he could nibble at it when he wanted. They were not that nice to eat and wanted the little fairy to get him some nice food. So he yelled at the top of his voice, "Mr Fluff!"

Mr Fluff could just hear a tiny voice yelling so loud in his tiny ear. He whizzed through the cat flap and out into the snow. There was snowman that Hazel had made. So he would have to whisk up a spell for that. He could see the magic hollow door. So he knocked on his own door and the pink snail opened it for him. Mr Fluff shot in and the snail told him that he needed some grub and fast as well! So off he went to the Witches larder and brought some cabbage leaves that she hadn't used and the snail was so happy that he gave the fairy a big kiss!

So off the fairy went back through the garden to try a snowman spell. So he waved his green wand about saying his words for a big fat snowman. All of a sudden the snow rolled into one big ball and then another one. So he needed the bits for the scarf and the hat. So he flew through the cat flap into the cottage to find a box of old clothing that Hazel was going to use for a snowman because she had mentioned this to her mother. Off he flew with the hat and the scarf to fit around the snowman and said some more magic words to make his face. The snowman looked pretty good. He wanted a bit more magic for him to speak. So he waved some more magic over the snowman with his wand!

Soon there was talking snowman and what a funny site that was. The little robins went to sit on this twig arms. Mr Fluff said, "oh it looks quite good here with all the twinkle snow to see if that white fairy had come in the night" The white fairy was busy covering the wizards garden with all his strange looking plants.

Mr Fluff shot in through the cat flap to enjoy the warm lounge heated up by the stone hearth. It was so cold outside and wondered that the snail was so hungry and was busy munching his cabbage leaves, that this would do him for a few weeks. He flew off to the big green tree covered in sparkly baubles that he loved to see his reflection of himself and how much he had grown! He was almost as big as one of those biggest red baubles Hazel had put on the tree. Some baubles were smaller than he was, and others where quite big to the little fairy. In a white glittery bauble made of tiny bits of silver glitter he could see something magic appear in the glittery bits. "Oh!" he said, "Another fairy's face" The face appeared and disappeared and he told the Witch about it.

"Oh, it's the fairy of that purple wizard with the magical hollow doors!" he must be very magical you know.

He talked to the face that appeared in the bauble."Oh where you magically created like me as a caterpillar?" he asked.

"Oh, I think that sometimes they are and sometimes that they aren't!" said the face in the bauble. She blinked her eyes at him.

Mr Fluff was also wondering how other fairy's came to be. As being changed into a caterpillar first had made him puzzled.

"That, magic rose had created part of you and the other fairies put a spell on you!" said the face in the bauble.

"What else does that magic rose do?" asked the little fairy.

Hazel said, "Oh it was here when we bought the cottage and the barn three years ago. I have heard a tale from the Irish Leprechaun that the rose belonged to the fairy queen"

"Oh and how old is the rose bush? He looked outside the window to see the rose bush had fallen into a winters sleep with the magic slowly fading into the snowy season. The snowman he had magically created had walked off into the forest whistling a tune. Mr Fluff didn't know a great deal of magic and the Witch Hazel would be teaching him some new things in the winter time. She thought that it was a good idea to have a fairy in ones red pointed hat! So she decided in keeping Mr Fluff in the house all through the winter. He soon discovered that the Witch had a lot of plants coming into her warm cottage house. That big sunflower had moved itself indoors so it could look out of the same window as the fairy could. The sunflower had a face on her. She was snoozing most of the time. She said once to the fairy, that she was an everlasting sunflower and the magic would last twice as long as the plants outside!

"Oh look outside Hazel!" he said with the big snowflakes falling from the sky.

He had not ever seen this much snow before and it looked like everywhere would be covered in 3 foot snow. The sunflower opened one eyelid just to pip at Mr Fluff glued to the old windows. There was a smile on her face, because she was indoors and not outside. The snow would kill the magic of the sunflower and Mr Fluffs didn't know what the snow would do other magical plants. The sunflower always slept most of the winter with the Witch even in her mother's old house!

Hazel was always rescuing plants from various places she wanted a big green house built in their daughter's garden. She hadn't done much to the garden for 3 years. So she was busy writing her cookery books first before deciding what she was going to do with the garden. She wanted to purchase some more land and that talking oak tree over the wall. So she had to wait till next spring to send a letter to the owner of the magic forest that she wanted some land to add to her garden. She loved collecting magical plants and other plants from different places and had a good idea of having a tea party in the garden.

Soon it was a special day when lots of her friends popped in to visit her on their broom sticks and the funny thing was they came when the snow had stopped. The next day as Mr Fluff fell asleep on a green bauble, something popped magically through the cats flap and you whom it was! It the new white fairy and a winter solstice present too. The fairy was very happy to receive to presents and see his new friend. That he couldn't wait to open his presents. So he waved his magic wand to open one present to discover a white musical box with a snow flake that made some musical tune. In the other present was a cosy orange sleeping bag made for fairies. He was very happy about that.

"What have you got then?" asked the sunflower yawning about her summer dreams of lots of birds wanting her seeds.

"Oh, a white musical playing box and I can sleep in the box with the orange sleeping bag!" So he demonstrated how he would sleep in it to the sunflower.

"Very nice of that rare white fairy" she commented. "I know something about a magic garden that has white roses. She comes from that magic garden that purple clever Wizard visits!"

"Oh, he was enchanted by the white fairy. "Where is this garden then? He asked.

"Oh, it's a secret place Mr Fluff and that rose bush actually came from that garden. The fairy queen owns that rose bush outside in that garden with all the snow outside. It is very old you know. Only that Wizard knows about that secret enchanted garden!"

There was more snow coming and the Witches friends left their presents to Hazel and her mother who was fast sound asleep in the bedroom her rocking chair with two fast asleep on the wooden bed.

Mr Fluff watched all the snowflakes fall onto the window sill and there was no sign of his snowman that he had made earlier. He looked at the big green tree with all the presents put under it. That she must have received a lot of cookery books and a new magic wand. The old wand had an old man's face on it. This also had ivy leaves growing around the wand. The wand made a remark about the other new wand. "Not much magic for me to do then? He winked at the orange fairy.

"Mr Fluff giggled, oh I'll come and play in the summer with you!" he said it quietly to the old wand. The old wand pulled a face at the fairy and the witch, that Hazel was so busy making magic for mince pies!" To hardly notice that the 200 year old wand from her grandfather had other special ideas of what magic it would do with Mr Fluff next summer.

She knew that wand was dancing on the cookery table dishing out a spell to light the old oven. That Hazel had a huge big present from her mother that was a new red oven. It wasn't quite yet and the snow still fell from the sky that Mr Fluff was feeling rather sleepy and dozed off again on one of the glittery baubles!

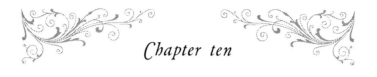

Chapter ten

MR FLUFF AND HIS WHITE SNOW FAIRY FRIEND

BY VERONICA KELLY

It was snowing very heavy after Christmas day. The witch hazel was enchanted by her new red oven and started to heat it up. She was planning on making some more cakes. Mr Fluff buzzed into the kitchen and he hadn't touched his cookery book for some time. He was so memorized by the big snowflakes. He was stood on the kitchen window ledge and so was the black fluffy cat looking out into the garden. It was rather a small garden and the witch wanted to purchase at least 2 acres of a big garden and a green house. Everything in her small garden was covered in 2 foot of snow. Something funny happened to some of Mr Fluff's magic on the snowman that he had created. The little small snowman waved through to Mr Fluff smiling as he ran passed the big

Oak tree. The snowman soon disappeared again into the thick snowy forest.

There was a faint glow coming in the snow and it was hard to make out what it was. The fairy had watched it for some time and the light got much brighter and twinkled outside the kitchen window. Then something shot through the cat flap and almost spun the other cat around bewildered, to what had whizzed past in a rush to get indoors!

The torte-shell cat meowed and spotted a very white fluffy glowing very brightly. "Oh, I come to visit the orange fluffy fairy!"

Mr Fluff went to see the visitor and he found out it was that snow fairy that belonged to that Wizard with the magical doors!"

"Hello!" he said to the snow fairy.

"Greetings, Mr Fluff, I have come to visit for a few days and it looks like more than that if it snows even more!" she said fluffing up her white wings.

"Thanks very much for your flying visit and the musical white box" he said.

"Oh, could do with a nice cup of tea then!" said the white fairy. She seemed very cold. The Wizard said it wasn't really a good idea to fly to the edge of the forest when there is a lot of snow forecasted. She said she would be quick in flying and she was too.

Hazel had put her mother's old copper kettle on the red new oven stove. So it would be awhile before the kettle would heat the water up to make a pot of tea. She had put her red tea pot and some tea bags in the teapot. The teapot gave a smirk at the fairy's looking at its decorative lid and what went inside him. She had many tea pots and they all went above the shelf in the kitchen humming tunes and singing wintry songs.

The white little fluffy fairy was cold and she went to warm herself in the lounge. She sat on the edge of a very old rocking chair with an old man's face on it. That rocking chair was smoking a pipe and the old magic wand was sharing the pipe with the rocking chair. The smoke made funny faces and the magic smoke seemed to disappear. Hazel told the chair to stop smoking his pipe! So the rocking chair said a magic word and the pipe had vanished in a puff of pink smoke. "You know I have been everywhere with her uncle. I love the summer so I can visit the great big bowling garden. I can smoke all I like watching old folk have a good afternoon!" said the chair to the two fairies.

Mr Fluff hadn't a clue to what the chair was on about. The snow fairy was only interested to when it stopped snowing so she could do one of her snow spells to show her new friend what she could do. He would have to wait till the next day as it was snowing rather a lot.

"Let's make a snow fairy white cake!" said the snow fairy.

"We would have to ask Hazel about her magic spell books. She has a lot in the lounge"

The two fairies flew into the lounge to look at some cookery books. Some were very old books indeed. Some of the books had eyes on them and faces. One had a face of a white fairy just like a snowflake. The white fairy had opened up her pages and a musical sound came from the book. Mr Fluff was quite surprised about the book. He turned the pages to gaze at the colourful pictures and said. "This one looks like a lovely icy white cake!"

So he fluttered his wings and buzzed around the house looking for Hazel who was sleeping on the bed with her two cats. She was too sleepy to disturb! So they fluttered after her mother called Lillian and found the old lady knitting squares for a big blanket she was going to make. She had lots of squares all piled up in her bed. "We want permission to make a white icing cake!" said Mr Fluff.

"That would need some of my cooking talent. Hazel's been to cookery school. I have been gardening!" she giggled. "Never mind my cookery skills are enough to get us started!" The old lady soon put her knitting away and tottered down stairs to sample some Rum before the cookery equipment out for making an icing cake.

The two little fairies were quite excited with Hazel's mother to do some cooking. She nipped to look in her cupboards to look for the ingredients for the big icing cake. She pulled out a rather big glass jar filled with lots of fruit all diced up. Then the icing sugar on the shelf she reached for. Then went into the kitchen and put them on the old wooden cooking table. A rather funny old cookery book yawned and announced to Lillian that he had some rather good receipts and winked at two fairies giggling. "My recipes for some rather gorgeous icing cakes are in my pink pages with lovely pictures if you would like to look at them! "She Said, the book with one eye open, and his little legs sitting over the edge of the shelf.

Lillian looked at the whole of the shelf where her daughter had put some of her uncle's old books. He had a big collection of books and she kept his cookery books before he sold everything in his house. The cookery book said he was not used for a long time for his spells in cooking up cakes. Lillian grabbed him of the shelf and looked up at some of his pink pages. A smile spread across the old enchanted book cover! Those two fairies flew around waving their wand's to turn the pages. "What a lovely gorgeous pink icing cake!" said the white fairy.

So it seemed that they were going to attempt to cook this pink iced cake. Lillian found a mixing bowl and put some whipped eggs in the bowl. Then she added some flour that she had measured. Then put the fruit from the jar in the mixture. There were some strange magic coloured bottles stored in a pantry with all the dusty cobwebs. Hazel had another collection of magic bottles and it seemed these were the ones that she used at her cookery school when she was learning spells for cooking. Lillian picked up a collection of rose red bottles with pink coloured liquid inside. She poured a few drops of liquid into the mixture and tasted the ingredients that tasted of a very spicy rose and added some other drops of pink liquid into the mixture that started the spell for the pink cake. There were also other ingredients like pink rose petal that made the ingredients change and pink smell of roses filled the air. Mr Fluff waved his magic wand over the mixture and pink magic dust scattered all over them. Lillian added other ingredients of magic pink and orange and the contents of the cake changed again and the ingredients was ready to be put in a cooking tin. So she went to find a good cooking tin and poured the ingredients into it. The oven lit itself and said it was ready to cook there cake.

So they had to wait over two hours before the cake would be ready. So the two fairies were whisking through the magic cookery book at some rather tasty cakes. The orange fairy liked the chocolate mint cake! "How wonderful it is to cook chocolate mint green cakes" he said.

"Oh, Mr Fluff we have lots of magic coloured bottles. One wintry evening we can have another go at that minty cake!" said Lillian.

The oven said the cake was cooked. So Hazel's mother whisked the cake out and said it would need some time to cool down. The cake smelled of roses and Mr Fluff grabbed a bit of cake and the magic cake turned his wings pink for a whole hour that he looked like a pink fairy. The white fairy took a bite to and she turned pink too. It was funny that Lillian nibbled a small piece of cake, and her hair turned pink. So they all giggled about it.

Later on in the evening they iced the cake and put some rather decorative pink flowers on it from out of one of the pink jars in the pantry. Mr Fluff couldn't stop waving his green magic wand at the cake. That more icing flowers appeared with pretty edible coloured ruby stones in the centre. Mr Fluff was sampling some of his spells he had put on the pink icing cake that made his wings changed colour to very different shades of pink and made them giggle all evening with fairy pink dust being produced by the magic fairy cake.

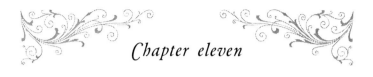

Chapter eleven

MR FLUFF AND HIS WHITE SNOW FAIRY MAGIC CAKE

BY VERONICA KELLY

A week later after they had cooked a magic pink cake the snow fairy wanted to cook a white iced cake what she was telling her fairy friend about. She had woken the mother of Hazel who was dreaming about what she should do in her daughter's summer garden. The sad thing was that the magic rainbow rose had disappeared and died in the snow with some magical remaining sparks like fireworks. Mr Fluff was very sad about his rose bush vanishing that the old pipe and rocking chair told him to stop sobbing and fretting about an old rose bush! The chair new about a secret garden in the forest and said when it was summer they would show the two fairy's some gorgeous rose bushes. Hazel had decided to go out with her mother in the afternoon for some shopping.

Mr Fluff had got his orange wings back after a week of nibbling the pink cake they had made last week. He also was playing with his white musical box that the white fairy had given him as a Christmas present. He spent some time at night winding the musical tune that sometimes it woke Hazel up in the dead of night to make a pot of tea and go back to bed. She knew Mr Fluff didn't do it on purpose. He was just a playful fairy.

Mr Fluff and his white snowy fluffy fairy both went into the pantry to get some ingredients for the white cake. There were lots of coloured bottles and there was a white transparent bottle with some very white glittery magic stuff in it. So the white fairy had whizzed that off the shelf into the kitchen. The cookery book with all lovely cake recipes in it magic pages woke up and danced of the shelf while the other were fast asleep.

He turned his pages to find a very white icy cake and floated into the air to find the two giggling fairy's. He soon found them in the pantry collecting magic potion bottles. They had a big collection on the table of different potion bottles that glimmered there magic. Mr Fluff found some rather good Christmas cake filling left over that Hazel had made. He put a spell on it and tipped a few essence of a bottle with petals in it. He was finding all sorts of things to add to the ingredients for the cake mixture. The white fairy added some glazed white cherries along with some red ones. She had found other magic bottles with orange petals and glazed orange rind. The white fairy was wavering her magic wand about. Lots of white orange sparks were coming from the end of her white wand. Mr Fluff was laughing with such fun, while the two witches were out shopping in the snow on their broom sticks.

They spent a good deal putting all sorts of ingredients into the white cake that by the time the two witches came back with lots of shopping and warned themselves out! That those two little fairy's had fallen asleep on top of the cookery book with the pink pages. A face appeared on the cookery book in the form of a rather delicious pink cake with hearts on it. The King of hearts was fast asleep with a smile that he had told them to cook a cake that would be cooked for a rather royal occasion with all the fancy ingredients. He was quite an old cook book and he had come from the secret garden where Hazel uncle used to have competitions in cooking the fanciest decorative cakes. This time this cake would be rather snowy.

"Oh look at what these two little things have been up to!" said Hazel

"How funny and nibbling bits of the pink cake we made the other week" said Lillian.

The book woke up and yawned . . ."We have been busy making the ingredients for a white cake with all the decorative bits. We thought that we would wait till you got back to light the oven. I don't wish to singe myself!" said the cookery book flapping its pink pages.

Hazel lit the oven for whatever those fairies and that cookery book had told them to put in it. They had been using her old bottles from cookery school. She had been out with her mother buying new magic spell bottles for some cooking and they came in a big wooden case. It was quite a struggle flying on her broom stick and a spell for the stuff she had bought for the packages to follow the broom stick pointing with a twig in the direction of the cottage!

The red new oven was lit and their magic cake went into the oven for a good hour. Hazel was busy unpacking what she had bought. She had bought some rather decorative cake tins and some cooking tins in different colours especially some bright red ones to go with her red kitchen.

Lillian had made some tea with a rather talkative red teapot. "They have been giggling all afternoon with that white magic potion they poured in the ingredients and I wonder what kind of spells they put in it.

The snow outside was coming down faster that something flew through the cat flap and it was a tiny green fairy all cold with the snow! Mr Fluff wondered who it was and flew to have a look.

"Oh, it's cold outside and I live far away from my hollow tree deep in the forest. I saw a bright light in the snow and found a rather nice cottage!

"Oh never mind" said Hazel. "We almost got covered in snow shopping. Have some tea!"

So the little fairy flew on top of the coloured orange sofa with the cat fast asleep on it. It was quite nice to be out of the way of the cold snow. He waited for this cup of tea and a bit of pink cake. She said to the green fairy, "That it's a bit of magic cake!"

"Oh" said the green fairy with a smile.

He tasted the pink cake and there were round pink spots forming on his green wings. He thought it was very funny. "There are lots of other fairy's in the forest that are unable to get back to their hollows!"

"Oh dear" said Hazel.

She had no idea that during the night that her cat flap would be visited by lots of fairy's that got lost in the snow. It was well into the evening when Lillian ventured outside with a glow lamp and stuck a spell on it. It was quite a very bright light and the fairies would see something glowing. It wasn't long before she had some fairies come through her cat flap in the door. That the torte-shell cat was quite surprised of how many winged visitors he had got in the late afternoon all wanting to get warmed up in his fluffy fur. The black cat also had a lot of fairies of different colours all riding his back. That Hazel must have counted over 30 fairies!

"That cake of yours is done in the oven!" So Hazel took it out of the oven to stand in the kitchen table. It smelled very nice indeed. It would take awhile to cool down so they could add the icing sugar on it. The afternoon soon became very dark and it still kept snowing and more fairies were coming!

"Oh! What a surprise" said Hazel, with lots of fairy's buzzing around her nice warm cottage? The white fairy was busy getting all the ingredients for the white magic icing. The cookery book was astonished to find lots of fairies in the kitchen feeling rather hungry. So Hazel was quite busy making a spell for small tea cups to appear out of nowhere to make lots of tea for the fairies with lots of other cake on offer. As she thought that magic pink cake would be too naughty to turn them all pink. She had some other sponge cakes with chocolate coloured buttons on them. The fairy's sat there eating bits of sponge cake and getting warmed up. "We cannot get our hollow trees" they all spoke in such tiny voices.

"Oh never mind . . . . It's awhile till the snow clears" said Hazel.

Mr Fluff was totally excited with these fairies in Hazel's cottage. He was the only orange fluffy one amongst them. A little blue fairy said she knows who he was! And it was her that turned him into a fluffy fairy with some rather funny magic! The magic rose helped as well that changed the fairies magic.

Soon the cake was ready cooled off and she said to the fairy that Mr Fluff could be ready for making the icing. So the excited little fairy tapped the cookery book and it too tottered off and jumped onto the wooden table with the tea pots making lots of tea and Hazel making a fairy spell of little tiny china cups appear. These little fairies would have to spend at least a week in her cottage till the snow had melted away. The old Oak tree was glowing like a pink lantern. The musical door had played its tune in the snow. Mr Fluff could hear it even in her cottage.

"Oh I am so excited about the icing sugar" he said buzzing his orange fluffy wings.

The other tiny fairies were drinking tea and nibbling at some of the bits of cake that Hazel had put out. The cookery book opened its pages for Mr Fluff to look at the recipe for white icing sugar. He needed some egg whites and a lot of icing sugar sifted into a big funny faced bowl. Too large eyes looked at the orange fairy sifting the dusty sugar in its bowl. Then he dropped two egg whites and put a spell on an egg whisk. So it was whisked lightly and Hazel had to help finish it off. She was good at spells in making the right kind of icing. The fairies insisted that they help to. So it wasn't long before the icing went on the cake with a little snowman that Mr Fluff had managed to make with his magic wand.

"Oh what, a nice looking icing cake Mr Fluff"

The little fairy waved his wand again and the glittery eatable decorations scattered on the cake. Soon they had a tea party with the white fairy cake. The snow fairy waved her wand and it looked quite pretty with a bit of tinsel wrapped around it.

During the evening it got very dark. The only thing that glowed was the oak tree that was quite aware of the snow that kept coming. A lot of fairies had flown in that night. It seemed that Hazel and Lillian would have to entertain them for the rest of the week with making cakes and spells for lots of tea. So Mr Fluff had a good time with the other fairies making cakes and he was soon sleeping on the book shelf where the other cook books were. He was dreaming about what other cakes that the old pink cookery book would show them.

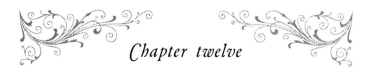

Chapter twelve

MR FLUFF AND THE BLUE BELL FAIRY IN A MAGIC GARDEN DOORWAY

One day when the snow had all gone Mr Fluff flew out of the cat flap and followed the black fluffy cat. The cat meowed and jumped on the wall that some workmen were going to start knocking down. Hazel had got permission to buy an extended piece of land in the forest. The sun had just peeped through the fluffy white clouds with spring around the corner. He did learn a lot about making all sorts of different cakes.

He sat on the wall and the Oak tree and yawned so loudly, and shook his branches that you could see he was coming out of his winter sleep. There were many tiny buds on his branches. He opened one glowing orange eye to see that little orange fairy wondering what kind of adventure he would get up to. He fluttered his wings and buzzed around the tree and knocked on his own hollow to see if that sleeping snail had woken up.

True enough that pink snail had grown a bit bigger. He was now as big as an apple. "Oh" said Mr Fluff. "You have grown quite big over the winter with all that snow we had"

The snail smiled because it was becoming a magic snail and he could still talk to the fairy. His big eyes looked up at the orange fairy. "I'm so pleased that the sun has melted all the snow. I can pop out and about to see what food there is on offer. I don't suppose that any rose buses have left me anything to nibble at?"

"To early Brian" said the fairy to the snail. "I am out to exercise my wings"

So off he went fluttering in and out of the trees. There were a lot of pine trees, Oak trees, sycamore trees, willow trees, silver birch trees. What he discovered was some very blue delicate flowers all under a willow tree. He fluttered near them and you could see the flowers tiny face. They heard him buzzing and looked up at the orange fairy. "It's one of the blue-bell fairies". They all giggled because they knew that one of the blue bell fairies had put spells on certain caterpillars in the forest. He stood to attention while hovering over the blue bells. Then a blue bell fairy popped out her head and giggled at him. "Come and see our magic secret garden!"

So being a bit adventurous he followed them deep into the forest. He really didn't know how to get back either! A strange door appeared with a key and his fairies opened it. He popped inside the secret garden. He could see people like Hazel having a nice tea party with lots of cakes on offer. So he flew near them and darted between the funny looking tea pots. "Oh mind where you go tiny fairy!" shouted the tea pot as he was about to pour some tea into a china cup. A woman looked up with a funny looking pink hat with lots of beautiful flowers on it. She looked at the fairy and tried to shoo him away. Mr Fluff wasn't too happy about being not wanted and buzzed around a little girl tucking into a cream bun. "Oh look a tiny little orange fairy!" she whispered. "Would you like a bit of cream bun. I really don't mind. It's my mother's Birthday party. She loves eating cakes and lots of things like coloured jelly and sweets"

"That would be nice "He said to the little girl. "I could not stay long as I got myself lost!"

"I shouldn't worry about that. I have a broom I could find out where you live with a map. Let's go indoors and play with some of my toys. I have lots of them including musical dolls and jewel boxes. You can see my tiny miniature pony called Bubbles"

So Mr Fluff went to look at Bubbles her tiny little fairy pony. He was busy nibbling at his pony nuts for his afternoon snack. He also had a red apple to eat for his tea. It was soon getting a bit darker as it was a well into the afternoon that he had discovered he had been gone quite a long time. Now that it was soon time for him to sleep in his own hollow with Brian the snail. So it seemed when he finished looking at the fluffy pony there was a bigger horse called Mr Snowman. He was big and white all over and pulled a horse carriage for the owners. He sometimes came out during the week and weekdays going into the town away from the big forest.

"So what's your name? Asked the fairy

"Oh, my name is Katie. I have another sister called Susie. She is older than me and goes riding a lot in the forest. I like to go riding with some friends"

"Let's go back to your house. I'm feeling rather tired now!" He said wanting to fall asleep. He would soon fall asleep on bubbles the little tiny pony.

Katie picked up the tired little fairy and popped him in her pocket and disappeared back to her mother's house. By the time they had got back it was very dark indeed. So the little girl waved her magic wand to see where she was going. She opened the front door with a magic spell to get in as her mother was in the kitchen cooking pasties with cheese. Mr Fluff soon woke up smelling the pasties and the cooking. Katie rushed up stairs and put the little fairy in the doll's house. "It is soon my dinner so I would get you something to eat if you like"

"Oh that's very good of you Katie" he yawned in the dolls bed.

Katie was off and running loudly downstairs to have her dinner. There were quite a few pastries on the table. She was pretty hungry too. She needed also to do some school homework. She brought out her school book they were learning about things in the forest. She did a little project on tiny mermaids in someone's lake. She drew pictures of them and they were all in different colours. Mr Fluff had not met any human witch like children. He only knew Hazel and Lillian who cared for him in the winter months. He was a bit fidgety with the dolls bed and it felt rather funny sleeping in a dolls bed. There was a porcelain doll with a talking spell. Katie had given her doll a name called Victoriana. She was dressed in a very pretty pink dress with flowers on it all embroidered. The doll fell asleep on the chair shutting her eye lids.

Katie was busy doing a spell for a magic ball to see tiny little mermaids in the lake. The crystal ball turned very green and murky. Then the crystal ball cleared and you could see a lot of little mermaids swimming in and out of the reeds. Katie was trying to draw some with her coloured pencils.

A blue bell fairy flew through her window to try and find Mr Fluff. She saw him having a kip in the dolls bed. "Oh there you are!" "I have to take him home tomorrow" her tiny little voices squeaked.

"Oh, its tiny Blue bell" said Katie. She was waving her pencil trying to draw something in her project homework book. "Look its Blue Bell" said Katie. "What do you think to my tiny little mermaids?"

Blue bell looked rather tired at Katie. She had been flying about looking at the newly hatched caterpillars" "Awe I've seen the mermaids in the lake sometimes in the evening with fish" she said. "I've been looking for wriggly things" she giggled. She would make more fairies with her blue bell wand. She had made Mr Fluff so I suppose she was his maker in a way. She was a gorgeous blue and purple fairy and often visited Katie and her sister. The fairy sometimes hopped on board the tiny pony called bubbles when he wondered in his field in the summer. Bubble was a little pony with a white fluffy white mane. Blue bell was not the sort of fairy to make any sort of cakes like Mr Fluff was learning of Hazel. She was a clever little fairy that made quite colourful magic and sometimes would put spells on things to stop them from fading away. Her secret was she was created by the rainbow queen. She had many creations of many beautiful fairies.

Mr Fluff woke up after his short nap in the dolls bed. The funny thing was when he woke up the doll popped in her bed to sleep. "Oh what are you doing?" he said to Katie. Katie was still drawing the mermaid.

"I have a school project on lakes and ponds. So I have to draw everything that I can find them. I have not gone swimming in the lake. My mum said it's not a good idea to do that. I would have to take the small boat with my Dad when he comes home from work. He won't let me row on my own"

The blue—bell fairy waved her wand at the crystal ball to show that orange fairy about the location of another magic rose bush in a secret garden guarded by elves. It was the same garden that the rocking chair knew and the magic wand belonged to Hazel's old uncle. "You need a secret spell and a secret key for magic door. "I could show the secret garden that lies beyond the emerald gate in the forest" "Maybe you could find a young rose bush to replant where the other one had vanished with its last piece of magic. Those rainbow bushes are very rare. That one that was Hazel's garden was over 300 years old!"

"What a very brilliant idea!" he said. "That would be a good project for me to get another magic rose bush. My pet snail Brian loves eating the rose bush when it sheds its luscious petals"

The moon appeared in the crystal ball showing some strange night creatures and one mermaid sitting on a rock splashing the water's edge. Then a little mermaid smiled at the fairy looking inside the crystal ball. She started blowing magic bubbles then popped back into the lake and her tail made a splash!

The little girl said, "You can stop awhile. I can take you home anytime you want to" she said to the orange fairy.

Mr Fluff yawned and found himself dozing off on one of the child's books. The little girl called her blue-bell fairy appeared again giggling. The little girl said she would put the little orange fairy in another empty bed in her dolls house. She had to hide her fairy friends as her mother was not one of these people to approve of fairies in her house. "Good night" said the little girl. Then a little tiny voice also whispered "Have nice dreams with mermaids. I will have them with blue-bell fairies!"

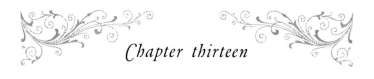

Chapter thirteen

MR FLUFF AND HIS NEW MAGIC UMBRELLA

BY VERONICA KELLY

One day it was raining in tiny little droplets. He was sat on the edge of his hollow tree. The spring had arrived and sometimes he would visit that Katie in the magic doorway. He had flown back on her broom stick the other week. She was very good with flying. He wanted to have something like an umbrella that Hazel uses in the rain. He was so small that he would have to have one specially made. His friend Brian the snail had already shot out the hollow door and the down the bark of the oak tree humming because he loved the rain so much. He was singing in the rain and all the other snails could hear him!

Mr Fluff didn't want to get wet, but he made a quick dash for the cat flap of Hazel's door. He came in wanting an umbrella and was asking the cookery book that was snoozing on the shelf for Hazel.

"Oh, it's that orange fairy!"

"I would like to see Hazel?" he said.

"She is upstairs snoozing. She is looking at the plans for her new garden wall"

So he went up fluttering his wings to see if Hazel was awake. She was asleep thinking how much she was spending on her new garden wall. The workmen had removed most of the wall. It meant his pet snail got into her garden rather quickly. He was always looking for something delicious to have and he sometimes found it. He had spotted some strange plant shedding some rather lush petals from ivy that magically flowered in the snow. Now it dropped the ground, the white flower had died. The snail ate the lot!

Well Mr Fluff fluttered his orange wings at Hazel and he could not wake her up so he found himself flying into her mother's bedroom. She was sat on that old rocking chair singing songs about rain drops. The little fairy stopped to listen.

"There were little tiny droplets on my crystal ball. They all shone different colours, and they made all twinkling sounds!" she said singing it.

"I wondered if you can make a spell for a tiny person for a tiny umbrella" said the fairy.

Hazel's glasses almost dropped off her nose. It was so funny. "I have not got a magic bright green umbrella!" she said. She was looking in her crystal ball still trying to hum a tune. "Along comes an orange fairy, fluttering his wings making a buzzing sound!" she said singing, "Wanting a tiny umbrella" she song.

"I'm sorry!" he said. "I came to see if I could wish for a magic umbrella and shake the magic droplets of my wings!"

"Oh, those have to be purchased with some money for such items!" she said to the little fairy looking somewhat like a tiny child.

"I've no money for anything and I also promised Hazel some money for that musical door way on my hollow" said Mr Fluff.

"Well you're only so young for an apprentice for help in her kitchen. So when you have learnt a bit more she will give you some pocket money!"

"Oh I am only 4 years old. I like making green and mint chocolate fairy cakes with all the icing decorations on it" he said to Lillian

Lillian smiled at the tiny little thing hovering and looking out of the window in her bedroom at the rain. "Watch this spell!" she said and waved her wand out of the window. The tiny droplets of rain changed to all different colours of the rainbow. Then a rainbow appeared at the end of the garden. The workmen stopped to gaze and joke about any hidden gold at the end of it.

"Oh lets go for a quick flight with my magic green umbrella to the shop that makes them!" she said to the little fairy.

So Lillian got her green spring coat on and fetched her magic umbrella and her broomstick. Off they flew up about the clouds and she waved her wand to cast more rainbows and the little fairy was quite surprised at the number of rainbows that Lillian could wave her wand!

They soon arrived at a shop at that sold all different colours of umbrellas and they were meant for witches and wizards. Some umbrellas were very colourful indeed. So Mr Fluff explained to the shop keeper that he wanted something very small.

"Oh, poor little thing!" he said, "I have some dolls umbrellas for you to have a look at" The shop keeper got about twenty dolls umbrellas to show to Mr Fluff.

"Oh, I like the bright orange umbrella" he chirped. He picked the umbrella up and tried it out. He seemed quite happy with it. So he wanted this one and not the others.

So Lillian paid the money for the umbrella, and off they flew home to her daughter's cottage. Lillian had put a floating spell on his umbrella and he would hang onto the orange handle and float all the way around the kitchen and the lounge. Then he had a go outside and floated around the garden and up the tree to his hollow. Oh, it was so cold outside in April that his tree house wasn't warm enough for him to sleep in.

Chapter fourteen

MR FLUFF AND THE NEW MAGIC ROSE BUSH

BY VERONICA KELLY

One morning Mr Fluff was sat on the new brick wall that had been done by the workmen. This took them a very long time to do all the bricks and they almost changed colour with the rain cloud that Lillian had put a spell on. They laughed a lot at the wondering cloud the other week. The cloud had disappeared into the forest raining all different colours of the rainbow!

Some of the bricks had changed a funny colour of red and orange and further down were the bricks where blue and purple. Then near the past the tree was a bright green and another blue. So Mr Fluff chuckled to himself all about that cloud she had put a spell on. It had been raining all week in the forest. There was no sign of the two girls he made friends with. Something else was rather funny as well and that was the thatched roof. The roof had changed colour with the rain drops that cloud had done. Poor Hazel was standing in the doorway thinking of getting her new roof done. Well it was different colours and the fairies in the forest said the old lady spell worked up a treat. Hazel had paid a lot of money for the roof to be done in a summer's afternoon in June. There was nice work going off in her garden. They had put all the plants in pots that were taken up from the ground. She was having a nice new grass lawn put in. The gardener was busy whistling to himself and making pots of tea with Hazel. Hazel started to smile a bit.

"Good morning!" said the gardener to Lillian.

Lillian had popped out to see where that cloud had gone. "Ahh spells like that only last a week at the most with my garden magic!" Giggled, the old woman.

The gardener looked up into the sky with his mug of tea. The cloud was near a pond just over the far end of her garden. Mr Fluff hadn't yet discovered it. They had a lot of snow this year and the pond was frozen over. It was only a small pond and Mr Fluff thought it was a puddle!

"Well now!" said the old man laying some bricks further down. "My Mrs is good garden magic. She never did anything as funny as your magic! So I'd never thought of putting a spell on a cloud!"

"Just a bit of fun Mr Caramel"

"What nice coloured bricks" said the orange coloured fairy to Mr Caramel.

"Why that is a fluffy orange fairy" he said.

"Yes, he belongs to my daughter" said Lillian

"Not to long before this wall is finished this end" he said.

Mr Fluff looked at the wall and suddenly decided to buzz in doors and ask the magic wand and the rocking chair about that secret place in the woods for a new rose.

"We could ask Lillian about that" said the chair.

The chair called Lillian in doors and she was a bit surprised to be talking to her daughters uncle chair about a trip to that magic place were there are a lot of roses that are sold. It is where they had made cakes in competition and had a very big supply of magic rose bushes for sale. So Lillian decided to go along with it and find the secret place of her brother.

So it wasn't long before Mr Fluff and his friends had all decided to leave the cottage and the workmen to find this magic place. Lillian had got her old broom stick out and the rocking chair with a funny mans carved trees face on the wood. The magic wand had slipped into her hat with Mr Fluff riding inside an emerald green hat with lots of pretty coloured stones in it.

They were flying high above the forest and spotted that rainbow cloud again delivering its coloured rain drops over the forest trees. You could see sometimes the other tiny fairies of the forest dodging the cloud. Some butterflies had been caught in the rain and turned them into tiny rainbow fairies with its magic! The cloud had a face on it by now and saw Lillian and decided to follow her into the secret doorway of that emerald gate. The third door on the right led to the secret garden. Not far were the two little girls had lived. They lived next door to the other secret garden.

You had to open the door with a key. So the old wand had turned himself into a magic key and opened the door. They all shot into the secret garden. This had included the cloud following to see if he could water some roses along the way. The door shut behind them and they were left behind the door with a strange big rose creeper that had completely covered the wooden door. You could not see the door handle unless the wand had shouted "Door Handle!" and that would appear through all the thick roses and creeper that covered it. Mr Fluff buzzed about and you know what. He had forgotten his magic umbrella! Though, Lillian did not and popped out her bright green umbrella for everyone to go under.

There were lots of strange big plants in the garden and Mr Fluff was looking at the big sunflowers that had grown and they were peeping through some of the big other coloured sunflowers that were a very bright yellow and orange. "Look at these!" he said to Lillian.

"Why yes, my daughter has one of those. She likes sitting in the lounge in her pot so she can look out of the window!"

"Mr Fluff then decided to get wet in the light drizzle and the cloud laughed at them and disappeared into the hedge with a rose maze. The cloud made lightning bolts and the poor fairies dived into the biggest green house that they could find. This meant even Lillian on her broom stick did the same and off she went indoors with her bright green umbrella.

Inside the big green house there were other strange looking folk having some kind of garden party and selling all sorts of cakes, Jams, Teas, Fruit, Sweets. "Isn't it a good idea to have some nice tea and cake and buy a rose later?" she said to the others.

The only thing that was going to have tea and cake was her and the tiny little fairy Mr Fluff. He sat down on her that then and found himself sitting on a tea cosy. It wasn't long before Lillian was making herself very happy with all the tea and a nice rose cake with lovely pink icing on it.

"Have you thought about what kind of magic rose you had in mind Mr Fluff?" she asked.

Well Mr Fluff was excited because he had always wanted something that did magic things. So he really thought hard about what this rose bush would do. He missed the old one that maybe this one should be different to a rainbow one. After all that the rainbow cloud, was soon running out of his magic power that his raindrops were having less colours in them. He would be back to being a naughty cloud in the forest were Lillian lived. Maybe if he asked her in the spring time he could do all that naughty things again. Maybe that he could drop his coloured rain drops around the forest and on Hazels thatched new roof!

"I would like to visit the rose garden" he asked Lillian.

"That isn't too far from here. We have to follow the footpath and the sign posts"

So Mr Fluff ate a crumb of her lovely pink rose cake and a small bit of icing sugar. He was offered some tea in a dolls cup that Lillian had brought with her in her small purse. The little fairy loved tea and especially the one that tasted like a sweet tasting orange. In which Mr Fluff like all sorts of teas especially from Lillian's collection from China and India. She had holidays in India sometimes and would bring back all sorts of teas. This time she would book a holiday and maybe take Mr Fluff to some exotic land to visit. "They have such beautiful flowers in India" she remarked to the little fairy.

Lillian was soon ready and off they flew through the winding flowery footpath into a strange green and white glass house full of roses of all types.

Mr Fluff flew amongst such delicate scented roses that smelled very sweet. Their magic was tiny little white icing flowers floating as the flower shook its head to produce sweets. In which Mr Fluff tasted one to eat. The sweets were collected by other white fluffy fairies putting them into wooden baskets. He went to other roses looking at what kind of magic they did. Some of them made cakes, different scented petals for bottles of colouring liquid. Mr Fluff could smell something like perfume from a very strong pink purple flower. She turned her head around to look at the fairy.

"I can see an orange fairy. There are white and pink fairies here in the green house. I get visits from very strange folk indeed like elves that collected our beautiful petals that last for only a few weeks. I like making perfume for ladies and they go in magic blue sparkly bottles. I do spells and turn things into other things! I best am placed in someone's big garden so I can talk to the other rose bushes and flowers" she said to Mr Fluff.

Mr Fluff had to attract the attention of Lillian who had parked herself with her broom stick and umbrella on a bench. Mr Fluff said he found a magic pink and purple rose who does spells and makes bottles of perfume.

"I love perfume" she said. "I have some money to buy some plants and she went off to pick up this pink and purple bush in its pot. There was something very small curled up in a ball and you know what it was! A tiny baby white fairy! So she popped her in her small bag and said to Mr Fluff, she was coming home with me. So she bought some other small plants and off they went back through that secret door with all the plants. She could hear the tiny white fairy sobbing. So she opened up her bag to have a peep and said, "It would not be to long before they arrived at our cottage" The fairy was only one years old and had no other friends. She did not want to work in the big green house collecting petals off roses. She wanted to live in a forest like Mr Fluff did.

They arrived home at Hazel's cottage and the rain cloud had followed them back and chuckled to himself he was almost out of rain! So he fell asleep while the sun came out the other clouds. Mr Fluff popped out of the green hat of Hazels to play with a new play mate.

"Oh and what is your name?"

"Petal" said the rose and she was a very white and soft pink fairy. She knew nothing about spells like Mr Fluff had learnt. That she would have to learn something about petals and looking after them. The elves had set the fairies to work collecting petals and that is all she knew. She even didn't have a wand! How sad that was. Mr Fluff said she could borrow his in the summer and play in the hollow. He boasted about his tree house and his magic about lovely cakes he had made. The tiny little fairy looked up at him. She hadn't grown that much in a year. Mr Fluff was 4 years old soon. He was thinking about his birthday cake.

"Let's have a go at making my Birthday cake" he said. "That would be another day, as mine is in April"

Chapter fifteen

MR FLUFF AND HIS MAGIC BIRTHDAY PARTY

BY VERONICA KELLY

In the kitchen Mr Fluff was putting all his mixture of his favourite green colour magic potion in the butter and icing sugar. He also put some green flour in and stirred it all up. The magic produced some stunning effects of green sparkly lights. The tiny little pink fluffy fairy called Petal had sat on the red teapot lid blowing bubbles out of a magic bubble bottle. She had been there for a week and seemed to watch Mr Fluff the orange fairy at work in the kitchen. They were good pink and green bubbles and they popped and disappeared after a while.

"Oh look" said Hazel. "Isn't he busy making his own magic cake?" I hope my hair does not turn green this time!"

The old lady looked up at Mr Fluff through her spectacles because she had to keep an eye out for fairy learning about certain big cake with such powerful potions to pour into them that everything he put in it. She had to look at the label.

A few eggs went in and he made a spell for the whisk and it beat very fast for Mr Fluff and sometimes the whisk got carried away. So the old lady had to do it for Mr Fluff. Sometimes he needed some help with it. He also popped in some glazed green cherries and there seemed to be a big lump off them. He jumped into the sticky mixture and licked his lips with such sugary taste. "How lovely and sweet these petals are!"

The fairy called Petal buzzed off the teapot to see he had flown into the cake mixture and became covered in the sticky stuff that he offered to give her a taste on the end of a silver spoon. Petal reached out and daintily took some with her hand and licked it. What a nice minty taste as he had poured some of that magic green potion stuff with the flour and margarine in. The old lady had fallen asleep for her mid afternoon snooze. So Mr Fluff was busy trying to get out of the mixture and get some more magic bits to stick in it. He had found a whole jar of chocolate buttons and he put all the green ones in it.

Soon he was putting some other green sweets into the mixture and they were melting into the mixture. He soon thought that the mixture had enough ingredients and woke Lillian out of her snooze for her to pour the mixture into a baking tray. She awoke out of her sleep and saw the two little fairies that they had finished with the mixture of the green cake. So she poured it all into a big cooking cake tin, then she popped it into the oven for a good hour and half. He soon had to make the icing mixture for the cake. So that he had to have another clean mixing bowl for his green icing sugar. So off he popped and poured lots of icing sugar into a mixing bowl and added one egg yolk with the help of Lillian who had to separate the egg yolk. Then they were mixing it all in and he poured a very bright green essence of colour to the mixture. Then he added the mint taste out of a very strong green glass bottle with a glass fairy as the stopper. Lillian smiled with all the magic new bottles that her daughter had purchased in the Christmas fair. There were many colours of bottles with different stoppers on them. All made out of glass and Hazel liked to keep them on her shelf so she could see them. One bottle was of a mermaid sat on a very green and blue liquid. That her liquid would be used to turn icing bright blue and conjure a magic spell of a ship riding the waves and then the magic would disappear!

Mr Fluff flew amongst all the magic bottles looking at all the different stoppers and they all seem to move with a bit of tiny magic. One hour and half later his cake in the oven had cooked. He could smell the mint already. Lillian brought the cake out to cool and Mr Fluff was excited over this big spongy green cake. He waited a long time before he could put some icing on top of the sponge cake.

He soon waved his magic green wand with his star on it and all the icing sugar drifted out of the bowl and landed on the sponge cake. Without making any mess at all. He was getting very good at doing cakes. So he waved his magic wand again and empted a magic green bottle full of eatable shiny green stars. The stars scattered all over the cake and it looked quite pretty. Then Lillian had popped some tiny little candles on it. They were tiny enough with a magic spell for fairies. It looked quite nice and then she put his cake in the lounge on a table. This little bit of magic with the candles was only meant for a short time, so that the flames wouldn't melt all the wax candles that she had put on it.

"What about the tiny balloons?" he said looking up and around the lounge. Lillian opened a packet of tiny balloons and had to use a lot of puff to blow them to their size and they seem to float in the air as he waved her wand.

"There are different colours" he said.

"Yes they are you had better call in all your fairy friends then!" she said.

So off he went through the cat flap visiting all the trees with hollows in and giving the fairies in invitation that he had a Birthday going on. He soon had a lot of other forest fairies coming and Hazel and Lillian had a house full!

Lillian had decided to buy him a miniature table with a tea service so it would go in his sleepy hollow. It was created for dolls tea party, but it suited little fairies as well. It looked rather nice all wrapped up in a box with a big green bow. Now Hazel had bought him a writing set of pens and just for fairies. It would be nice if he learnt a bit more to read and write like most folk do. He could write all his spells down in a note book and colour in his pictures.

Mr Fluff came back with lots more friends and they all sampled his green sparkly cake. Lillian had also done some spells to make some small sandwiches. He loved cheese, and there were all sorts of cheese sandwiches. He also liked the strawberry jam sandwiches followed by mint green sandwiches. The fairies bought him some presents. He got new orange jacket and a pair of orange wellingtons. They all seem to match his bright orange umbrella. He had also a bright orange waterproof hat and he tried them on. He looked like a little miniature boy with bright orange hair.

"Oh I have to look in the mirror" so he turned to look at himself in the mirror and he found it funny. He was the brightest orange fairy of that forest!

His friend Blue bell bought him a tiny magic book on the creatures of the forest. He opened it up and it was a popup book. There were many fairies of the forest and other strange creatures that flew. In the pond were the tiny little mermaids all collecting hidden gem stones that the elves hide under trees making wishes.

Mr Fluff went to open his box with the bright green bow. Inside it was a bright green tea service. It was on a dolls miniature table and he said, "Wouldn't that look good in my tree house!"

Lillian had saved some carpet in her bedroom. She loved green emerald and small piece would fit in the tree house. She told Mr Fluff that she would have to climb up the ladders to get to his hollow. She thought that would be a small treat for Mr Fluff. She never thought what the tree had said about his two hollows. The other fairy was going to get the one right at the top! It would be a while before Petal his roommate would get sorted out in hers. She liked to play with Mr Fluff. So he liked his new orange wellingtons.

The fairies enjoyed the cake and the sandwiches and the balloons had popped by late afternoon. Both witches were having their sample of Mr Fluff cake. You know what was funny about that cake? There had turned very green and sparkly for a few good hours! Mr Fluff also turned a very bright green when he tasted his own cake that the other fairies giggled about it.

He went and flew through the cat flap outside and you know what! It was still raining all different colours. That magic cloud had been about dropping the rain drops and he saw the new thatched roof that the workmen were still laying it in bits. There were no workmen at present because they had all gone home for tea. So they had left part of the old thatched roof on, and the other half with the new thatched roof. It did look funny with the rain dripping into the stuff they had put on the roof to make it thatched. Mr Fluff had no idea that they were using some sort of special wheat. He took one look at the cottage and buzzed with his wings to find some puddles to jump in!

"Splash!" he said as he found a big puddle and it was a bright green puddle.

Then he went to the other puddles splashing those. The rain cloud had made lots of different puddles of all colours. After a while he went flying with his magic orange umbrella and it seemed some fairies were sheltering under big toad stalls of different sizes. They were magic toad stalls and Lillian said not to eat them because you could very well turn into something else other than being a fairy. So he kept to eating things at home except the clovers that sometimes appeared in the summer. They made him grow much bigger. He was about 3 inches tall and the other fairy was so tiny, that she fitted into Lillian's small green bag for outings. She was only one inch tall and had a lot of growing to do.

He soon found a very big lake on his travels that was bigger than the small pond right at the back of Hazel's cottage. There was a barn there and lots of hay and straw there and something was very big munching away at its evening meal. So the little fairy went to have a look and found a rather big grumpy shire horse in its stable. Moaning that there were no carrots for his tea and the farmer had forgotten to give him his carrots. So Mr Fluff went inside the barn to have a look. He floated about with his umbrella and spotted a heap of carrots that the old horse was moaning about. That he could not get any for his tea. So the little fairy went to see if he could ask the horse weather a few carrots would do.

"Hello!" he said to the horse. Mr Fluff was sitting on top of the stable door.

The horse looked about not actually seeing anything at all. Then he spotted something buzzing about on his stable door. "Talking miniature folk" grumbled the horse.

"I am small, but I can get you a carrot!" said Mr Fluff.

"Maybe we can share some carrots!" said the horse and his ears went forward with some delight.

So off went Mr Fluff and put a spell on some carrots and they moved about bobbing in the air to the horses food bucket. There big carrots dropped in and Mr Fluff found a very small carrot indeed! So he tasted some carrot and it was very good.

"Thanks very much then!" said old Jack the horse.

"That's ok then. Oh I better be back home" he said to Jack.

"Do you live with someone?"

"Oh, I live in a tree house and I stay with hazel and Lillian"

"I am alone here at night. No friends at all except the farmer who gives me work to do. You have to come around again we can have a natter and a nibble at those carrots"

"Good bye then" and off he flew so quickly in and out of the trees and over the big lake. There was some very big fish look at him and disappear in the deep water. There were different bits of coloured water droplets floating on the surface and a little purple had popped up out of the lake to see where that naughty rainbow cloud had gone.

He was soon flying back home and Hazel was wondering where he had gone! He rushed through the letter box instead of the cat flap and wanted to tell her about the big Shire horse called Jack. He was still soaking wet and he still had a baby carrot in his hand. Hazel was busy with the goody bags for the other fairies. They had no idea where he had gone.

"Oh Mr Fluff you should be playing with your new wellingtons and umbrella!" Hazel said.

"I did" he said. "I didn't go far" he said with a smile munching his carrot.

"That be old Jack, he went to visit" said Lillian. "That horse is cutting the wheat for my thatched roof. He's grumpy with it and is soon for retirement in a field somewhere. Old Jack's owner is after a young mare at the shire horse show!" said Lillian.

"Oh am not that interested in horses Lillian" said Hazel.

"My father was and your uncle was. So I guess our fairy friend is too"

Mr Fluff dried off his wings and went to help himself to some fairy cakes. "Can you make a carrot cake?" he said with his mouth full.

"I think you can" said Hazel

"Well I have to get some more carrots off the farmer then?"

All the other fairies giggled about the orange fairy finding old grumpy Jack without his carrots! This is because the old farmer was getting old himself. Lillian smiled about it. Mr Fluff was eating some bright orange cakes that Hazel had conjured with her wand. The only thing was that they were just a bit of magic and tasted like sweets out of a liquorish magic box.

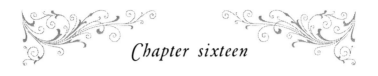

Chapter sixteen

MR FLUFF AND HIS NEW MAGIC MERMAID FRIEND

BY VERONICA KELLY

Mr Fluff found himself sitting on the edge of a very big lake. He could see his tiny face in the reflection. That he had grown quite a bit with all those nice cakes he had cooked and used magic last winter. He had very bright orange hair, and eyes.

Something moved at the bottom of the water that he was looking at. Then something surfaces. She had a tiny little face and green long hair. She wore a pearl necklace that was really small. Then she popped out of the water and sat right next to Mr Fluff.

"Oh an orange fairy!" remarked the green small mermaid. She flipped her tail at him and teased the fairy.

Mr Fluff was spell bound at such a creature no bigger than he was. He was quite used to seeing magic people about like Leprechauns, witches and wizards. "Oh, and what kind of magic person are you? He asked.

"I'm a magic small mermaid. Some folk capture us and put us in there tropical fish tanks!" she giggled. She was only teasing him.

"What is your watery world like down there? He asked.

"Would you like to take a peep?" she giggled again.

Mr Fluff could not find himself to get wet in the water. He gave it some thought that fairies don't go for swimming lessons. He knew that he could not swim.

"Oh I would get to wet!" he said.

"Oh, but I know of a magic spell that can turn you an orange merman for one hour only!" she said with a pearl wand wafting about.

"Are you sure that you're quite capable of such magic then?" he grinned.

"Oh, I'm very good at doing magic spells for some fairy folk like yourself" she said. "Want to see what happens!"

The mermaid waved her magic pearl wand and soon turned into an orange looking merman with a big fish fin tail. He soon slid into the water and found himself trying to swim. "I've never done this before" he said to the mermaid. She grabbed hold of his tiny hands and made a safe spell for him under water. He found that he could breathe in the water and he could see the fish that were swimming past the dense reeds that hung like green curtain trails. She was taking him to her little sunken ship. It was a boy's toy at one time she mentioned. It was a copy of a tiny frigate ship. She had collected a lot of sea shells on her travels. She gave one to Mr Fluff because it was a bright orange one.

"Can you here us sing inside this shell?" she said. "All the mermaids in this lake sing a watery song. This one is for you!"

He picked up the orange shell, and there was no snail in it. He wondered what his pink snail friend would make of it. It was quite true he could hear the noise of tiny little voices and swimming fish singing along. "That would be nice to show to my two witch friends" he said to the mermaid. She also gave him a pearl necklace to wear. There were also other little mermaids of the bottom of the lake all singing and collecting things and saw the orange merman! What a funny thought because he was really a fluffy fairy and some of the magic was beginning to wear off. So she took him to the surface and pulled him onto a big large pebble. Mr Fluff was wet!" He soon got his fluffy wings back though! They were wet too! So he decided to hang like the moths and the butterflies to a willow tree. This was to dry his beautiful orange wings.

"Oh look it's an orange fairy!" said one of the green mermaids.

"Too right!" he said, "I'm very wet. So I'm off to have a snooze while it dries off in the sun" he was under a very big leaf and so was some other butterflies that he winked at them. Then shut his eyes for a nap.

Two whole hours had passed and awoke yawning. He did feel very hungry and it wasn't for cakes and carrots. It was something else that fairies usually like to eat when no one is about. All he could think about was this juicy red golden delicious apple that Hazel had bought a basket full of them! All displayed in the kitchen ready to nibble at by very tiny mouths. He didn't think that the magic forest would have such red juicy apples. No one around here really would tell him of places to find them. Hazel brought many different fruits home and it was sure the summer. Most of it had come from abroad and she flew on her broom stick to a lot of magical places. Other than red apples he liked the French golden delicious as well. He wondered if there were any fairies in France. France was over the English Channel and was too far to fly, for a small fairy.

"How about nibbling at those wild raspberries!" said a rather odd looking black fluffy caterpillar with a pipe in his mouth. He made a very pink smoke around some of the raspberries and the smoke had put a magic face on the fruit.

Mr Fluff had fluffed his wings and saw the black fluffy caterpillar with his magic pipe. "I've never had any raspberries" he said. "Although I will try one" So off he did. He picked one and they were quite a fruity taste. That seemed to stop his tiny tummy from grumbling. He ate another one and another one. Till he felt there was not hungry anymore. Then he smiled, because he wanted another snooze. It was something he liked doing in the wild magic forest. The huge black fluffy caterpillar had a lot of legs. He had lots of boots to wear and off he went trooping off in the undergrowth.

Mr Fluff was dozing near that pebble again. His mermaid friend had popped out of the water and waved her wand for some magic. She appeared to be a very small person like Mr Fluff. She came to surprise him with her laughter. Mr Fluff was dreaming again. All those things, he dreamed about at the bottom of the lake, with a small frigate ship, and some mermaids swimming around it. The lake was all inhabited by tiny mermaids and strange looking fish.

"Mr Fluff!" she nudged the fairy into steering out of his sleepy head. He was quite full from eating those lovely raspberries.

"Oh, it's the magic mermaid. What kind of name should you be known by?"

"Call me pearl" she said. "I'm always collecting stones to put in my home" she said.

"Mr Fluff looked at his pearl necklace. They were very tiny pearls he noticed. He remembered Lillian had a fancy to a string of pearls with such a creamy colour. She had a lot of jewellery and most of it went into a big musical box. He had his musical box parked on the window ledge of the cottage that belonged to Hazel.

"That's nice name" he said.

He picked up the bright orange shell and put it to his ear. Sure enough he could hear some mermaids sing songs. He told her he would put it in his sleepy hollow. He said, "Would you like to visit my hollow tree for the rest of this afternoon. I could pick you up and carry you to my home!"

"Yes that would be a very good idea!" she said waving her wand.

Mr Fluff picked her up and off he flew in and out of the trees in the forest. He did live to far away. He flew pass the grumpy old Shire horse. Who was busy sunning himself in the field, lying on the ground. The horse heard a funny buzzing sound. He woke up to see what that naughty fairy was up too. Mr Fluff had missed a few nights, not delivering his favourite carrots without the farmer knowing his fluffy friend had done it.

He soon found his nest and flew in. The pink snail was snoring his head off till night time. He wouldn't stir from sleep unless it rained. The magic cloud had gone deep into the forest asleep while the sun was out. So he hadn't been anywhere at all today other than hovering above some ones house!

"What a small place you have!" she remarked. "You only have a big sea shell and a wonderful musical door" she commented.

"Please play us some musical chimes!" he said to the door.

The door played every tune its enchanted voice could think about.

"I like the pirate tunes!" she giggled. "We don't get pirates in these forests you know. There all out at sea!" said the tiny mermaid.

"I've seen the sea with Hazel. I got that enchanted shell on my travels with her broom stick!" he giggled at her.

"You need to collect some things you know Mr Fluff for your tiny little hollow house!"

"I did think about it pearl. I wanted a bit of a carpet in it. I think

"Lillian was going to give me a bit of green carpet soon!" he said.

"What about a table?" she asked.

"I have not had it put in my hollow. I had a Birthday party the other week. I got some nice things. They are all at Hazel's cottage. You can see Hazel's cottage from here. They are extending the garden for a few acres I think" he said.

"What does that coloured green stone do?" she said. It was inside the shell.

"Ahh, I have got it when I went to visit a man with a collection of gem stones. So I have the Malachite green stone. I make a spell and it keeps me warm some times in my hollow. I spent the winter with Lillian and Hazel"

"I escape my pond in the winter!" giggled the tiny mermaid.

She had a secret place where unicorns gather. "There was a very sparkly green warm stream there. The water has its enchantment and never has anything in it that dies. The unicorns had become sacred to the water. Have you ever seen one?"

"No I have never seen a unicorn. What are they?"

"They are white magical horses with horns" she said.

"I stay in their magic waterfall"

"One day you would have to show me this magic waterfall and these unicorns that you speak of" said Mr Fluff.

"You need to collect things for your hollow. These glow worms share your house!" She could see them hanging from the ceiling with a sleepy face on them.

"I better take you back. You seem to be changing back to being a mermaid!"

So off he flew and took her back home. It was a good thing too! Then she changed into a green mermaid, and went 'splash' into the lake. He buzzed above the lake and saw her flick her tail. Then she surfaced to say "Goodbye". He blew her a pink kiss with a fairy wand. He'd forgotten to kiss her! He had become a forgetful fairy. He flew back to his hollow and sat outside listening to the tunes of the magical door chime. He could see that Hazels house was looking very nice with the new thatched roof. It couldn't be long before that rain cloud with its coloured droplets of rain would pay a flying visit. Poor Lillian had got one of those funny spells on the cloud that was a bit difficult to remove. So the naughty cloud would make a quick dash if Lillian was out on her broom stick waving her hand to chase after some magic that wasn't really intended. Mr Fluff gave another yawn and he was soon fast asleep. The pink snail woke up to have a look outside. He was quite hungry and he knew just the place to get some grub!

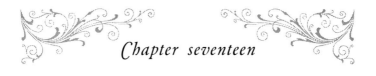

Chapter seventeen

MR FLUFF AND HIS PIRATEFAIRY FRIEND GINGER

BY VERONICA KELLY

Mr Fluff was sat on the new garden wall with all the different coloured bricks twinkling in the sunshine. That magic cloud had often sneaked around Hazels' cottage on occasions just to shed its rain in all different colours. Mr Fluff was learning how to whistle and the tiny little Robins had taken it with a joke that he squawked like a frog! He needed some lessons in the art of whistling and it wasn't going to come from the other chirping birds. He stopped for a moment and flew on the roof top of the cottage. You could see quite a lot from up here he thought. He could see Lillian with a pair of ladders. She had put them next to the old oak tree. The old tree opened one eye to look to see what she was doing. Then shut this eye because he really liked to snooze in the late summer. Lillian was playing door chimes with the magic door and after awhile it opened up to reveal a fairy's hideaway place "Oh" she said. "Looks like a bird's nest! Well with what she said, the pink snail woke up and said that Mr Fluff hadn't got around for any decoration or much decorative spells!

"I'm putting him a piece of green carpet in and some dolls to make it more comfortable for him" said Lillian

Mr Fluff felt a bit surprised that Lillian had managed to get to his fairy pad. It wasn't much at all. He still had this magic shell in it and he could hear the songs of the sea in it sometimes. Other than Lillian, that he could see from the roof top he could see the farmer with his new horse called Cherry. He went to flutter to words the farm and find the older horse eating his beloved orange carrots. He was getting an older horse and must be about 25 years old. He could hear the farmer whistling tunes. Then Mr Fluff tried to copy them very hard. It was rather true what the birds had said. He croaked like a frog! The farmer stopped whistling his tune as merry as he could be. "Oh I have a lovely red apple tree, and the old dear bakes me apple pie!" he said.

"I have a friend by the name, Old Jack!" said the fairy singing a tune. He did not whistle this time. His friend was the Old Shire horse in the old barn.

The old farmer stopped what he was doing with the horse's food bucket and his hands where rather deep in the beat pulp and the bran. He liked mixing the stuff because it smelt rather good. The horse always got a good meal late in the afternoon. The Ferrier was soon coming around to shoe the other horse called Cherry. The young mare had a smile on her face as she noticed that Jack had a fairy friend that used to sneak out in the late afternoon making sure that Jack had got his orange carrots. That she may promise him a ride of she got a magic apple from the old woman's house a bit further away from the forest. You see that the farmer and Mr Fluffs friends lived fairly close by each other. Other places you had to fly out of the forest. There was an old woman not far she had an apple orchard. She had a wine making business and the fairies used to come and help her with all the apples. The horse Cherry had known about the place because she went passed it on route pulling a rather big cart full of thatched stuff to put on peoples cottages.

Mr Fluff had not seen the farmer's new working horse yet. She made herself known by making a loud neighing noise. Something else popped out of the basket full of apples. You know it was another little naughty fairy with a very pirate outfit on. He was nibbling at a very rosy red apple and suddenly spotted Mr Fluff sat on top of old Jacks mane. Mr Fluff was wand wavering again and trying to sing a tune. He made the black horse's mane full of sparkly glitter and the horse sneezed!

"Oh look what we have here lurking amongst the horses!" said the pirate fairy.

Well Mr Fluff wondered who that was and stopped his wand wavering. Then flew to the stable door of Jacks and sat on the edge. He was looking around till he saw something buzz in the air. This fairy had wings with skull and cross bones. He had his little boots with buckles. He wore an eye patch and a pirate hat. He had a little shirt with frills. "Who are you?" asked Mr Fluff.

"I'm called ginger" he said. "After, Ginger Ale!"

"Never had any of the stuff" said Mr Fluff.

"I could show you where you could get a drink of Ale from!" said the pirate fairy.

"That's a nice thought. I come to visit Old Jack the Shire horse"

"You like the horses then? I love travelling in a pirate ship!" said the other fairy with some mischief. So the other fairy soon fluttered his way out of the stables to show Mr Fluff an Inn where he got his Ginger Ale. It was such a long way out of the forest. That Mr Fluff had to spend the night in the Inn. The barman gave them a drink each, in a tiny glass toy cup.

"We don't get many travelling fairies in Inns this end of town" said the barman.

"I live in the forest near a cottage" said Mr Fluff licking his lips on the Ginger Ale. "I live the Oak tree in someone's garden! The workmen have built a wall all around the tree and made a bigger garden for Hazel"

Both fairies were full with the lovely taste of the Ginger Ale. Mr Fluff had never tasted anything like this before. He usually drinks tea with Lillian and Hazel.

"You're new to all this fine stuff on offer!" said the Barman. "Try some Liquor it would clear your throat" said the barman.

So Mr Fluff tried some mint liquor and already felt the difference in the taste of things and his vocal chords. He could sing and whistle better than the Robins. It was all rather funny though.

"Have some potato chips with crinkly edges!" said the other fairy buzzing around the food on a shiny wooden table.

So off he fluttered to sample the crinkly chips and found out he loved them quite well. He liked his lips as he liked the salt and vinegar on them. He soon was quite full with the chips and ale he sampled. So was the other fairy who had found him in the horse's barn.

Both of them snoozed on the bar and Mr Fluff sometimes watched all the strange folk come in and have the food and a song and dance till early in the morning. The barman had picked both tiny fairies up and put them in a room upstairs that was usually let to travellers. The barman had collected all sorts of things to do with travellers with horses. He had a lot of leather and brass stuff hanging from the walls. Mr Fluff had found a nice cushion with flowers printed on it and fell deep into a sleep. While his pirate friend was sleeping on the window sill looking at the rain drops fall down. He was crafty fairy and wanted to be friends with the bright orange fairy. You see orange fairies are quite rare and often lead to treasure! So he had a magic pirate ship and a map and wanted Mr Fluff to find a treasure chest on a sailing adventure. He looked at his map with the magic words . . ."You must find a magic orange fairy of the magical forest!" Then take him on a short pirate treasure hunt to find your fortune!"

The pirate fairy soon fell asleep dreaming about his ship and his small pirate crew of 10 naughty fairies. They all wanted to make their fortune. He wondered what he could offer in return if he could find something as a little present.

The next morning Mr Fluff and Ginger had woken up in the Inn. So they let themselves out to go down for early morning breakfast. The Inn keeper had spotted them flying around the bottles on the shelf. They had different liquors all different coloured bottles. One had a magic gypsy caravan and horse inside the bottle. It was sweet orange taste and the pirate fairy was buzzing around it like a bumble bee. The Inn keeper said, "That pirate fairy always wants the sweet stuff!" so he opened the orange bottle with it and dropped a few drops on the edge of the spoon. The pirate fairy had sampled the lot. The Inn keeper was wondering what the orange fairy might want for his breakfast.

"I would like some tea and cake" said the orange fairy buzzing about the brass kettle stuck on a shelf on the wall.

"Now then, you're not a tiny lover of drinks then?" said the inn keeper.

"I like my tea" said Mr Fluff.

So the Inn keeper made a pot of tea in fancy teapot with a big smiling face on it. It was a blue tea pot with blue flowers on it. "Tea isn't bad in the morning" he said. The Inn keeper sat down with the other fairies. So Mr Fluff had his tea and a homemade cake with ginger spice in it. Then he was ready to go off with his pirate friend.

It wasn't too long that both fairies had left the Inn and the found themselves near a river. The river was so calm, it had a lock and a big shire horse pulling a barge. Further down the river was something floating on a blue fluffy cloud. It was a pirate ship!

So they found themselves flying on the pirate ship and Ginger shouted "Ahoy!"

"Ahh! Shiver my timbers. It will be our Captain Mr Ginger!"

Mr Fluff landed on a small toy Pirate ship being propelled by a blue fluffy cloud. It was floating just above the water down the river. Then it suddenly changed course and disappeared into a magical stream. Mr Fluff had no idea where he was at all with these fairies. They spent a whole week floating down the stream with all the dragon flies about. The giant frogs and toads hopping to one Lilly pad to another. Ginger had looked at the map to see where they were and said they had come close to the treasure in the water fall. Mr Fluff looked at the map with the treasure chest that was marked on it. He had to wave a magic spell so he wouldn't get wet. So he waved his wand and out of it popped a magical plastic umbrella that would only last an hour or two if he was lucky. So off he went flying under the waterfall to collect the treasure box and he saw it open full of gems and pearls. So he shut the box tight and turned the key to lock it. Then flew back to the pirate ship to show Ginger what he had brought back.

"Oh they're be treasure my orange friend!"

So they opened the box to find gold coins, a tiny glass crystal ball, exotic shells and some gem stones.

"So is this what you wanted then?" he asked.

"Yes it is. So we can buy things with it my friend and you can have anything out of the box"

So Mr Fluff said he wanted the tiny glass crystal ball. So they gave him the ball and the gem stone. So they sailed out again for another week drinking ginger ale out of a rather big bottle. It rained all that week to. So he was conjuring magic umbrellas to keep him dry from the rain. The Pirate fairies were singing getting wet and their ship suddenly shot off and spotted that naughty rainbow cloud. The ship hitched a lift and asked the blue cloud to sail on it. Mr Fluff was speedily coming home on that rainbow cloud.

"No problems my pirate friends!" said the rainbow cloud.

They were flying away from the river and back into the forest. Those fairies wanted to drop by at the Inn again. They said they had to take Mr Fluff home with his crystal ball.

"Oh, you mean that cottage near the Oak tree?" said the rainbow cloud.

"Yes, that's the one!" said Mr Fluff.

So the cloud disappeared with these jolly pirate fairies and they found his oak tree and two witches sitting outside with their cats on a new lawn fast asleep!

Lillian heard something and felt something like a rain drop. She looked with the corner of her eye and saw naughty cloud. She thought she would get wet so she jumped to her feet looking up at the cloud to see a pirate fairy ship pop out from the cloud. Mr Fluff had been gone for two weeks with the pirate fairies looking for some treasure.

He flew over the pirate ship and flew on his fairy hollow. The door sang a pirate song and then opened the door to let him in. So he popped his glass crystal ball on the toy table. Then popped his ruby gem stone inside the shell he usually sleeps in. He knew that Lillian had been in his hollow and he had a new table and a piece of carpet inside his hollow. The snail popped out of his pink shell and said that while he was gone that he'd been in the garden eating fallen flower petals of roses and he magical grown in the size of a golf ball. Well that was big for a common garden snail. His art of conversation was limited. "Where have you been?"

"Ahh, I'd been sailing down the river and down the stream, with some pirate fairies and a treasure map. I got a small crystal ball" he was quite chuffed with that.

His pirate friends had buzzed around his oak tree wanting to know where he lived so if they went looking for treasure again next summer. They would bring him along. So Ginger had made notes to where Mr Fluff lived. The pirate ship had woken up hazel. Hazel had never seen fairies with wings like what they had. They stopped the night in that cottage eating cakes and drinking tea. They were not that educated like Mr Fluff who could just about read and write. They were treasure seekers and kept the company of friendly Inns and pubs and clouds. Mr Fluff would have to learn to use that crystal ball. So Mr Fluff found himself asleep on the black fluffy cat. He started Dreaming about this travels.

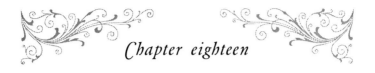

Chapter eighteen

MR FLUFF AND HIS NEW MAGIC CRYSTAL BALL

BY VERONICA KELLY

The tiny fairy had woken up from his deep fairy sleep. He popped out of his shell to gaze upon the crystal ball. He had quite a good time with the tiny fairy pirates and they said that he would be welcome every summer for a little bit of adventure in finding treasure. He knew that Lillian had been in his fairy hollow and put some carpeting down. It was a very bright green piece of carpeting that looked like grass in the summer. It worked out that Lillian's favourite colour was a vivid bright green! She had put a very bright piece of carpeting in her bedroom and this tiny bit was an off cut. So she had gone all around the edges of the hollow and it looked pretty cosy for a fairy's hollow. She had even given him dolls shiny wooden table and that made him very happy. He could use the dolls stuff for making things like the pots of tea.

"How about using that crystal ball!" said the pink snail that had slithered under the green carpet.

Mr Fluff scratched his tiny head wondering where the snail had hidden himself. "Brian" he called out. "Where are you?"

"Well see if that crystal ball can tell you where I have hidden myself!" laughed the snail.

So Mr Fluff put the crystal ball on the dolls table to gaze in it. He did a bit of gazing in it and you could actually see a rainbow cloud hovering above the cottage shedding some raindrops in different colours. "I can see only that rainbow cloud with a smile on his face" said Mr Fluff.

"You're not concentrating hard enough about thinking about a pink snail!" remarked the snail giving a yawn.

So Mr Fluff tried his best to think about a pink snail. So after a short while he peeped into the crystal ball and he could see a pink snail peeping out of his pink shell with a rather sleepy face. The snail was always snoozing on warm days and would not come out until it rained rather a lot.

"You love the rain Brian" It had just begun to thunder in the clouds with rather dull and grey angry clouds. "I will open the magical door" he said to the snail.

So the tiny orange fairy did open the door and it had played lots of fairy door chime tunes. The rain did come down like buckets of water. The snail comes out of his hiding place to have a look outside. He peered out of the door with his pink eyes to have a look. Sure enough everything was truly getting a shower of rain. "I'll just be off" said the snail. "By the way I've learnt to read a few words in those magic books of yours!" and off he slithered so quickly down the tree as fast as he could do it. He was in that Hazels garden looking for fallen petals from any of the flowers or roses. He had spotted magical rose bushes petals and they tasted ever so good! It was one of Hazel's new roses that she had planted out. It was a bright vivid red! The snail was now gone in the rain again.

Mr Fluff was left alone with his crystal ball and he kept thinking about things and they would conjure up what people were doing. Now, he thought about that grumpy Old Black Shire horse. That likes Mr Fluff so much that he would do anything for him. This is because he had made good friends with the horse with giving him the carrots, and he was now after the rosy apples in that rich woman's orchard. He could see Old jack the Shire horse looking out of his stable window at the rain. He had not been out all day he thought that his owner would let him out in the field at the back of the farm.

Now he could see the other horse that the farmer had called Cherry. She was out with the farmer on a round. She was 3 miles down a cobbled road trotting very quickly. The farmer had lots of thatched stuff in his wagon and it was on the way to another cottage to do some more thatching before the weather had changed. As you see it was at the end of the summer holidays and there was just a few weeks left of good weather to thatch a complete cottage. This area of forest was inhabited by at least five farmers with their animals and their crops. Cherry had now stopped awhile with the farmer to load the collection of reed thatch. He watched them quiet carefully for over a good half hour. It was a long time that they had unloaded all the stuff of for the roof.

Then he waivered his magic wand, to see what the crystal ball would do next. The scene changed to something else. It was that pink garden snail in Hazel's garden. He had found some good bits just lying on the ground of white rose that shed four petals. He zoomed over to petals and scoffed the lot. Well to that common garden snail it tasted very sweet in-deed. Never the less what else would a garden snail eat on his rounds! He slithered over to some toad's stools of a very bright red nature with white spots on it. It isn't that good to eat and so he looked for something else other than petals of rose bushes. No eating someone's plants in people's gardens was a naughty thing! He was told by the orange fairy not to eat any of Lillian's plants! I mean what else could one tiny thing eat? The tiny little snail smiled to himself at some other large big plants that were not doing much good because they actually had a bit of frost last night. So he slithered up the stem of this giant sunflower and began to nibble at the dying sunflower petals. "Not to good" said the snail.

Mr Fluff thought the snail didn't get to the good plants of Lillian would be turning his pet snail into something else! That is if she ever caught it on her prized plants.

Another wave of the wand and the crystal ball flickered deep into the forest. What a little surprise to see a mermaid combing her green long hair with a very tiny comb. "Oh it must be pearl!" said the fairy. He could see her with some friends and there was more than one mermaid looking at him through a crystal ball. There were at least four of them all in different colours. He had never seen a purple mermaid before. She had long purple hair that trapped deep into the watery depth.

So he wavered his wand again to see what else that the crystal ball might conjure up. You know he saw that naughty rainbow cloud with those tiny pirate fairies down another stream. They were all drinking liquor and they had been to that Inn Keeper again. They started to sing a merry song. "Were drinking Ginger Ale, and were floating down a stream, we spent our pennies on some tiny bottles of Ginger Ale and Rum!"

Mr Fluff shouted loud to the crystal ball, "We found a bright fluffy orange fairy, who found the treasure chest" and the words suddenly appeared in colourful fireworks display above the cloud. They all cheered and looked up at the words and carried on singing. "Were all rich pirate fairies on a merry quest?"

Mr Fluff looked into the fairy crystal ball and wished for something else. Do you hear a cry for help within the crystal ball!

"Oh help!" cried a fluffy pink caterpillar that accidentally had fallen into the stream.

"Oh look there is a fluffy pink caterpillar floating down the stream where those pirate fairies took me the other week!"

So off he flew with his magic wand to find this fluffy pink caterpillar making a plea for help. He flew a very long way indeed to find the poor fluffy pink caterpillar that had got into such danger. So he saw the little thing and flew down so close to the stream and plucked her out very fast.

"Oh" said the fluffy pink caterpillar. "I thought no one would come and rescue me and it would be the last of me" she said.

"Oh no need to worry I have a very cosy little hollow place where I live and soon we can have a cup of tea"

She was very wet and all her fluffiness was all soaked in the water from the stream and she was covered in pond weed! Mr Fluff had flown so fast he was almost out of breath when he made it back to the hollow. It went through all that naughtiness of all the chime tunes before opening the door. When the door opened he rushed in and popped her down on the nice green carpet trimmings that Lillian the witch had so kindly put in his fairy hollow for making it a nice cosy little home. "This is my wonderful fairy pad my dear little rescued friend" He opened his fairy magic book to find a very good spell for a little hand towel so he could dry her off with it. He waivered his wand and cast a spell that in the first thing that happened was all this fairy pink glitter appeared out of nowhere!

So he tried another spell that conjured a little hairdryer and magically without plugging it in as shown in his little spell book turned the switch for cool warm air to dry the tiny little thing!

"Oh I feel much better now!" said the tiny fluffy pink caterpillar. She was getting all nice and fluffed up with the magic hair dryer that Mr Fluff had fluffed his own wings with it as well. It was very funny indeed to see them both giggle and laugh at each other.

"Well I better introduce myself as Mr Fluff the rarest orange fairy of these woods" he said.

"Oh I was never given a name at all. I suppose we could think of one soon because I would go into a cocoon for the coming winter to be a very bright pink butterfly" she said.

"How about being a fairy instead!" he said. I know some fairy's that could make a magic spell and turn you into a fairy like me"

"That would be a very good present from a passing fairy like you" she said.

So off he went to find this magic bluebell fairy that was living in that ladies mansion house with the two girls that go horse riding. This little naughty fairy had taken two hours to find that place and he had found the two girls doing their school homework with all the spells that he had never seen for such young witches. The air was full of magic!

Katie was having a go at casting some green spell to make her hair go green for a Halloween party. She was also doing her homework with writing out the spell for her glittery green hair. Her sister was a bit older than her and she had got some homework about riding brooms and ponies.

"So what is the matter Mr Fluff?"

"I need a very good magic spell to turn a fluffy caterpillar into a fairy like the bluebell fairy did to me" he said fluffing up his orange plume wings. He had a big smile on his face. You could see that the fairy had almost run out of puff flying to get her secret bedroom window.

"I'll have a look for you. My tiny little orange friend!" so she shut her spell book and opened up the doll's house where that bluebell fairy was having a nap. She nudged the tiny fairy and asked her to spend a few days with the orange fairy and fly to his home.

"Good afternoon" said Bluebell. She had a long nap about dreaming of such crafty magic in the secret rose garden with the strange looking roses that those elves make such wonderful perfume with petals that drop to the ground.

"I need a small favour" he said. "I have saved this tiny fluffy caterpillar from an awful fate. So being in a good mood rescued her and I thought since you're the one who turned me into a nice orange fluffy fairy would do the sweet thing of doing a good spell maybe on a fluffy pink caterpillar!"

"Oh!" she said, "I love doing those spells!" Off she went to flutter her wings near the open window.

You know it took another a few hours to find his hollow. It was dark, as the nights were drawing in and it was mid

October. Lots of witches had made those huge lanterns out of pumpkins and lit there outside gardens with them. They could find their way home quite easily. They arrived at his door and both of them were out of puff again. The door opened and not a twinkly tune out of it!

"I guess you can spend the night in this nice hollow with me". He had made some cups of tea that Lillian had given him. There was this nice fairy cake on the table and a plum that Lillian must have put in his hollow climbing up her garden ladders!"

"Let's do the spell tomorrow then!" said the blue bell fairy.

"Oh, I am very tired!" she yawned to Mr Fluff. She took some of the fairy cake with the pink icing on and tucked into some tea.

Well the little fairy caterpillar had fallen asleep and had a very good natter with the pink snail. He said that Mr Fluff is a bit of a learner in magic! The fluffy caterpillar said she would wait till he had got back. She had curled herself into a fluffy ball.

Mr Fluff yawned and curled up in his magic seashell. The other fairy fell asleep on a knitted piece of blanket.

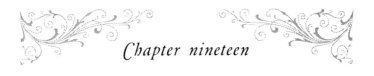

Chapter nineteen

MR FLUFF AND HIS MOTHER THE BLUEBELL FAIRY

BY VERONICA KELLY

*M*r Fluff was in his tiny hollow with a fairy that truly was his maker before he had turned into a fairy. He was just a humble caterpillar with a very big wish in his tiny little mind. He had wanted very big wings and he thought if he had eaten enough then surely next spring he would have them to flutter about the beautiful trees. He was living in someone's garden in a huge old oak tree that really took to having visitors at any season because it was where he was parked! Now the oak tree had become part of Hazel's big extended garden on the edge of the forest. Beyond the forest were vast acres of farming land where that old black Shire horse lived. He liked the idea of having these tiny little fairies so they would get him a carrot from out the big barrel the farmer had put them in.

He was just beginning to wake up and there was a knock on the door. The bell made a silly little tune because it was too early for Halloween. It was sometime next week when it was said that all spiritual beings came out in the dead of night to haunt the living! Mr Fluff never thought of such things as ghosts coming out for sweets or just having some fun.

He opened the door and a very blue fairy was fluttering her wings with fairy dust all over the hollow and the leaves on the tree had just begun to change colour.

"Can I be let in?"

"Oh, come on in to my cosy place!" said Mr Fluff.

He let the blue fairy in and she was much bigger than he was. She must be about three times the size of him. Mr Fluff was still a tiny fairy to the others.

"Have you anything to drink?" she said. "I'm kind of thirsty with a lot of flying from that girl's bedroom called Katie"

"Sure it would be some Ginger ale or some nice tea from Hazel's cupboard" he said.

The door shut and continued to play some Halloween tunes while they were having a drink of tea. Mr Fluff hadn't seen the blue bell fairy since the beginning of summer. She sat down on a dolls chair and had her tea.

"You have a very warm hollow then Mr Fluff?" she said. "I live with Katie in a very big manor house with the horses and ponies they have. Course I live in the doll's house!

"I like it here in my hollow and it is more a summer house. I stay with hazel and Lillian when the snow comes here" he said.

"Who looks after your hollow tree then?"

"Oh, the snail does. He likes the green carpet and slithers behind it sometimes to sleep in the dark before showing himself"

"I've come to put a spell on that pink fluffy caterpillar you rescued" she said.

"Ahh! She's all curled up in a ball near my sea shell" he said.

Blue bell got her magic blue wand out and started to weave a magic spell to change the face of the pink caterpillar. The pink fluffy thing awoke from her sleep to see a very blue fairy weaving magic. Soon she had a little pretty face of a fairy.

"That's part of the magic done!" said the blue bell fairy. "Now all you need is to collect some magic rose petals before the frost kills them. So you must hurry in her garden before there are no more roses!"

"Oh I would need some help with that Blue Bell" he said fluttering his wings and finding a tiny fairy bag to put them in. It had taken some weeks to make a fairy bag and Hazel had the old hand sewing machine out. He was never any good at fairy sewing so it was a good idea to use a spell for the sewing machine.

The magic door stopped playing its tunes and soon fell asleep while they went into Hazel's garden. Down they flew looking at what petals they were going to collect. He picked purple ones and white ones up. The bluebell fairy had gone to get some other pink petals in the garden. It was a shame that the other rose tree had gone.

"I think we have enough" she said. "Let's go back to the hollow tree and get the petals near the caterpillar she might eat them. Maybe tell her that she needs good wings to fly with. She must eat at least all of these before she goes into a very deep sleep and change in a chrysalis"

So there was a pile of petals near the pink caterpillar. The tiny pink lady caterpillar opened one eye just to gaze at what he brought. She started to nibble at some.

"Well that's done then!" said the Bluebell fairy. "Why not come to our house and have some fairy spells down at the manor house. "I'm sure Katie would give you a lift home on her broom stick"

So off they went flying into the woods to find this old manor house through the secret garden door in the forest. It was kind of unusual to find one of those doors because it was generally covered in vine leaves and the occasional white rose bush with its leaves around the door handle. The door opened by itself and they let the two fairies through to the garden. The big mansion place was a good 2 miles flight from the door. So that took over 30 minutes to get there. Naturally the other fairy always kept track of the time with a mini watch given to her by Katie. "Looks like it's getting very dark!" said Blue Bell.

"I would have to spend the night in the manor house then?" said Mr Fluff. "I can't fly out in the dead of night!"

"Never mind" she said. "Katie is quite a good girl and would let you stay in the doll's house I live in"

Soon they arrived at the big manor house and they found the big window open to the bedroom at the top of the house. They tapped outside wanting to be let inside. It wasn't long before Katie had opened the window latch to let them in.

"I see you have brought a friend in called Blue Bell" said Katie.

"Oh, it's a fairy I had made some 4 years going back" she said fluttering her wings at the girl.

"You come to do a bit of magic then. How about playing with the big crystal ball of mine!" she said to them.

Katie picked up a big crystal ball parked upon the fire place ledge. Then put it down on her bed and you could see its clear white crystal glaze. She picked it up again and showed them a little trick with the crystal ball. "Glitter ball" she shouted to it. All of a bit of magic there was silver glitter inside the ball and then she said something else to it in a twinkle tone. "Change your magic colour's!"

So the glittery ball had changed to a lot of greens and blues mixed in with reds. It looked very pretty with the different colours. She said something else to the crystal ball and it changed to white snowflakes falling in a nice little cottage with a man walking his pet dog.

"Now you have a try with the crystal ball. Mind you, little orange fairy, that my crystal ball is much bigger than fairy ones!"

So Mr Fluff whispered to the big crystal ball, "Fairy trees"

The crystal ball had conjured up a tree that looked like his in the woods with a fairy door. It made a Musial tune if you listened hard to the ball. Then it showed him another fairy door that wasn't his but belonged to an elf like fairy that had painted his all green. This elf like fairy was smoking a pipe and was sat outside his door on a branch smoking a funny odd sort of clay pipe with a tree and a spirit face etched into it. The elfish fairy saw a fluffy orange fairy in his green crystal ball looking through the glass at him. So he waved back to the fluffy orange fairy and smoked a little butterfly disappearing into a misty fog.

"How about doing some cooking spells Mr Fluff? Let's go down to the kitchen and have a go at making some strawberry ones. There are loads of strawberries all in a basket. I picked them the other day on a strawberry farm. That's the farm near the other one with that grumpy black shire horse and his owner!" Katie said.

So of they went into the kitchen to bake strawberry cake and lots of cream. The orange little fairy was quite surprised about what he was to taste and so was his mother Blue Bell. She licked her blue lips at the taste of cream and she liked the idea of ice cream as well. Mr Fluff had not sampled any of these foods before. So Katie had gone into the kitchen drawer and pulled out a silver spoon and then went to the fridge to get the cream out.

"Can I taste the cream?" asked the Blue Bell fairy.

"Oh alright then" said Katie scraping a bit of cream out of the bowl to give to the fairy.

The fairy licked all the cream of the end of the spoon. It was funny that Mr Fluff had eaten a whole strawberry with some gusto.

"Where is the cake mixture?" said Mr Fluff.

"Will come to that my tiny friend" said Katie.

Katie had decided it should be a sponge cake and started looking in one of the recipe books. She had come across the ingredients for the sponge, lots of butter, eggs and sugar. She weighed them all and put them in a magical whisker that whisked the ingredients. Then she added some pink colouring to the mixture. What you got was a very pink of sponge. Then he poured the ingredients into a baking tray. Mr Fluff kept waving his magic wand with all the edible glitter falling into the baking mixture. "You have to bake it for at least half an hour. So she did and while the sponge was cooking Mr Fluff was looking at the magic potion bottles. He said that Hazel had brought lots of different coloured bottles that did different things.

When the sponge was baked Katie had fetched it out of the oven. You had to wait till it cooled down. So that was another 20 minutes and Mr Fluff was licking his lips at the cream. "I've never had cream before!" he said.

"You wait till you have ice-cream in a different colours and tastes" he said.

"Have you any ice-cream that I could have a sample of?" he asked.

"Yes I have. The mint and chocolate one you can try. Mother bought it only last week"

So he sampled some ice-cream and he had to tell Lillian and Hazel about the stuff and soon it would be Halloween.

Katie poured all the cream on top of the pink sponge cake and added all the strawberries to it. "Come and have a taste!" she said.

Katie's mother appeared in a puff of purple smoke and her broom. "So your cooking for fairies then?" she piped.

"Oh, well I have a new fairy friend with us and I thought it was a good idea to do some cooking. She's one who bought the very old cottage. I bet she spent a fortune doing the place up. Lillian comes from a good working family but deceased"

"That's nice to know!" said her mother.

"Get your share Mr Fluff and then we can play in the attic with all the spell books that my Dad gave me" said Katie. "I'll take you home tomorrow morning and there's no school it's half term. Soon be having a Halloween party!" Katie said.

Mr Fluff looked rather funny with his tiny little hands holding a very tiny strawberry. He took a little bite and the taste was lovely. He buzzed with his wings all around Katie who was sneaking up the spiral staircase with the strawberry cake and shouted out for her sister.

All late in the afternoon they had eaten some of the strawberries. Mr Fluff felt rather full with the cream too. So he soon fell asleep on a rather large pot pumpkin with lights. He dreamed of a Halloween party with lots of fairies eating the strawberries and pumpkin pie.

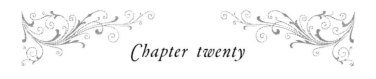

Chapter twenty

MR FLUFF AND AN INVITATION TO A HOLLOWEEN PARTY

BY VERONICA KELLY

One week later after Bluebell had been to visit Mr Fluff and show him around that rather posh mansion house. He was sat outside his musical door. It wasn't a bad autumn day, but the leaves were blowing all over the garden and over the wall. The old Oak was wide awake at this point as he found that Hazel was putting up some orange lanterns that she would light up tonight. The tree was quite happy being decorated for one night in Halloween. It was 200 years before anyone had decided to put any sort of decoration in his branches. He felt good that the big cottage had been sold. No one had lived in it for a good length of time. The only thing that used to visit the forest was the birds to nest in his hollow.

There was a purple broom appear in a puff of smoke. That broom belonged to Katie's mother. It had the fairies on the broom handle taking a lift delivering an invitation to a Halloween party. He had been given an orange envelope with a pumpkin sticker on it.

"Hello Mr Fluff. We come to invite you to that Katie's Halloween party. All the little kids from school are coming!"

"Oh, what a surprise!" he said. "That's tonight then?"

"There mother is paying for it all. She had spent a lot of money on the big pumpkins and there's a big cake made out of pumpkin. Lots of other stuff as well!" said the tiny little fairies.

"Oh what a nice surprise!" he said opening up his orange invitation. There was a spell on the card! It had a funny picture of a pumpkin and a witch flying on an orange broom. It made a musical note to Mr Fluff. "Come out you tiny fairies and let's have some fun!"

There fairies had whisked off to Hazel and Lillian. They had invitation as well and were quite happy about it. Lillian loved parties and had already thought of what she might wear at Katie's party. "Oh I have to make some more pumpkin cakes with orange on!" she said.

When it got dark Mr Fluff was being picked up by Katie on her bright green broomstick. She was whizzing in and out of the trees for the tiny little fairies to come and have a lift on her broom. You could see this bright lit broom with lights twinkling in the forest.

Hazel and Lillian had been baking all afternoon and whisked themselves on their broom sticks through the forest to get to that secret door and garden. It was very dark and spooky finding your way on lit broomsticks at night time. They hadn't seen any ghosts wonder in the dark forest.

They zoomed through the magic door and into the magic garden that was usually full of variety of roses. It was quite frosty that night and most of the roses had died off in the autumn. The only thing that was strange was the big toadstools that grew about a three to six foot height. They were a strange colour of red and white spots and the field mice wear hiding deeply in the hedges.

Mr Fluff had rather a long ride on Katie's broom with about three hundred fairies all trailing after the broom. They finally turned up at the big mansion that was very nice and a warm glow through the windows. The door was wide open and the broom and the fairies all shot in. They entered the huge hall and went into the big lounge were there was a huge table full of Halloween party food. Mr Fluff had seen his new friend there already drinking samples of that Ginger Ale. He had sailed by on his magical ship and had been invited by other fairies to join on the party. There was music playing on the gramophone.

Mr Fluff was very fond of cake and sampled some of the pumpkin cake for his tea. Then he fluttered across to talk to the pirate fairy ginger. He said he always comes to Katie's Halloween parties and her Birthday one. He said he always gives her a present from his treasure chest. This time he gave her a ring that was transparent stone, that you could see the changing of the seasons. She was wearing it on her finger and showing it to her friends from school. The children were very busy eating the crisps from the bowls and were waiting for a game to play. They had come up with hide and seek in the mansion house. Some parts of the house had signs up where they shouldn't hide. Some of the children were dressed as ghosts in white sheets. They were making all sorts of spooky noises with three wands. Sometimes it spooked Katie's mother because she was this posh upper-class woman.

Mr Fluff had never seen a musical gramophone before and had a go at changing the record. He found it very funny when he played it at the wrong speed. There was a song about ghosts and ghouls. He had no idea what a ghost was or a ghoul. Katie thought if she explained that when things or beings died, that they became ghosts and ghouls. That if she died that she would go around and haunt the forest on a broom. The broom said, "That would be a bit of a giggle on a luminous broom!"

She went to dress up like a ghost on a broom and whizzed around the house on it. So Katie did and her mother had turned a very funny colour seeing a spell like a ghost on a broom. Mr Fluff had learnt that witches only had fun at one time of year and called it the Witching Hour! So far he hadn't seen anything ghostly at all.

Katie had played for a good hour or so on her flying broom and so did the school children winning little presents when they hid themselves in a very odd places. Katie put her broom down and the broom hovered outside into the garden. Mr Fluff had eaten enough party food and had rather a long chat with that pirate fairy. He said that he came over every year to Katie's Halloween party. He said that he enjoyed retreat here because of the entire goings on with the magic forest. He said he found all sorts of treasure to be found in all sorts of places and it was good for trade when he went on his holiday abroad. He said the most things they looked for was rings and necklaces to put in their treasure box. His pirate ship was a good boy's toy. He had a clever idea to make a spell for tiny clouds. He found that the rainbow water cloud in the forest and got chatting to it. It however didn't really have any sort of conversation with any living thing other than its neighbouring clouds high above the sky.

He said that the rainbow cloud had told him he had been in that forest for centuries and the people that used to own Hazels cottage were well to do people of a farming produce. They had owned part of the forest and had a very good garden of such strange vegetables and they sold it to all sorts of people. They became old and eventually the odd couple had died and left everything to the forestry commission. The commissioner of that time had put a time spell on it. No one could purchase it at the time. It was well rumoured that the other previous people who owned the cottage in the 17th century were purple wizard and a White Witch and they disappeared in mysterious circumstances. The forest commissioner at that time sized the property.

"There you have it Mr Fluff about the owners of the cottage!"

Lillian and Hazel went house hunting and came across this cottage by chance looking through a catalogue of cottages around Derbyshire. Hazel inherited a lot of money from her uncle and she bought her daughter the cottage and purchased the old barn.

Now that, the cloud usually made its home snoozing on top of the old thatched roof. It was like having one's own bed! So Lillian found him quietly kipping on her daughter's roof top. She put a spell on the cloud to shift his fluffy body off! What a spark she made with one of her wands!

Lillian had a good collection of antique wands from her uncle. This one turned the cloud all different colours! So he would have to find somewhere else to park his fluffy body. He disappeared to that farmers place with the grumpy old Shire horse! He parked himself on the timber of the roof of the stables and the horse was well amused about the coloured cloud and the water droplets it shed! The horse tried to lick bits of the rain drops that dropped through the cracks and the ceiling onto his salt lick.

"How interesting!" said Mr Fluff to the other fairy. "Have you seen any real ghosts and goblins?"

"Would you like to see a ghost? asked Ginger. "I know of one that sleeps inside a tree and she comes out in the early morning hours and disappears into the spring lake!"

So Ginger went deep into the forest with Mr Fluff and some school children on their brooms. They promised to be very quiet indeed. They came upon that very tree that was wrapped and shrouded in leaves of a sacred vine and somehow ghostly white material. A woman immerged from her tree. She was very pale and very white and ghostly. She drifted about the old ancient trees wondering in and out leaving a ghostly luminous substance behind. Then she walked on water and began to disappear into its depth. There was a glittering like thing in the water. A lot of blue ghost balls came out of the trees and danced on the surface of the water. Mr Fluff was quite entranced over it.

The school children were spell bound to tell their other friends in what they saw. So they speeded up on their brooms and flew as fast as they could. Soon they came back to the mansion and the Halloween party. They shot indoors as fast as they could. This included a orange fairy who went to warm himself near the hearth. The children had seen a real ghost that they found it hard to explain to Lillian and Hazel. Mr Fluff however had found a cosy teapot after warming himself up and popped inside of it!

Hazel and Lillian were very busy having a chat about a gardening project for a glass summer house that would be very big in the garden near that Oak tree. That she planned to fly to lots of flower stores to buy lots of plants in the spring. That it was her dream to have a beautiful glass house with exotic plants from all sorts of places around the world. Hazel discussed that she would renovate the whole of the cottage on a project and have children come to do cookery lessons with Hazel in the summer. That entirely summed up what Hazel was going to do and Lillian.

As for Mr Fluff he had a lot of spell learning and reading to do. He was just a baby fairy. That he would learn that the fate of the forest in the future was hidden. There was treasure beneath the forest floor and a terrible fate of the forest would come. That the codex book was hidden somewhere and had to be found! The Green Witch was to be written in the codex book and a powerful spell to be unleashed!

Lightning Source UK Ltd.
Milton Keynes UK
UKOW04f0128040714

234552UK00002B/10/P